Baby-sitters' Island Adventure

Look for these and other books
in the Baby-sitters Club series:

Baby-sitters' Island Adventure
Ann M. Martin

AN
APPLE
PAPERBACK

SCHOLASTIC INC.
New York Toronto London Auckland Sydney

Cover art by Hodges Soileau

Interior illustrations by
Angelo Tillery

ISBN 0-590-42493-9

12 11 10 9 8 7 6 5   2 3 4 5/9

Printed in the U.S.A.   40

First Scholastic printing, July 1990

*This book is for
the mascots of the Lunch Club:
Kathryn and Michael,
Christian and Callie*

I thought finding the secret passage in my house was exciting. I thought going on a cruise through the Bahamas and then visiting Disney World was exciting. I thought sneaking into a graveyard on Halloween night was exciting.

I thought my parents' divorce was traumatic. I thought moving from sunny California to snowy (in the winter) Connecticut in the middle of a school year was traumatic. I thought getting a stepfather and stepsister was traumatic (and exciting).

I was right about everything—but that was before my friend Claudia Kishi and I got stranded on an island with four children. Now *that* was exciting and traumatic. I still can't believe it happened. Claudia and I set out on a sailing adventure with my younger brother, Jeff, and three kids we sometimes baby-sit for -- Haley Braddock, who's nine; Becca Ramsey, who's eight; and Jamie Newton, who's just four. We never thought our dream trip would turn into a nightmare.

But it did.

Haley said the adventure was sort of like being in one of her favorite books, _Baby Island_, by Carol Ryrie Brink. In that book, two girls are traveling on an ocean liner that gets shipwrecked, and the girls wind up in a lifeboat with these four babies and have to live on a tropical island practically forever before they're rescued. At least Claudia and I didn't have to take care of any babies. A lively eight-year-old, a nine-year-old, my brother, and Jamie were plenty. And at least we didn't have to wait _too_ long to be rescued, although I must admit that the length of time we were on the island seemed like an eternity.

While we're talking about books, I should also mention that _Jeff_

2

said the adventure was sort of like being in a book he had read in school that year. The book is called <u>The Cay</u>, and it's by Theodore Taylor. I read it once, too. I'm glad our experience wasn't as harrowing (or as long) as the boy's was in that book. Still...

My adventure was the best and the worst thing that ever happened to me. (So far. I'm only thirteen. I assume that better and worse things will happen if I live long enough to let them.)

Since being stranded on the island was so exciting and traumatic, I decided I wanted to have a record of it. Of course, no one ever <u>expects</u> to get stranded on an island after a sailing trip, so I didn't have a pen or any paper with me. In order to have a record of the experience, I had to rely on my friends' memories, letters, diaries, and notes from the time I was away, and also,

of course, on Claudia's and my
memories. As soon as we got
home, we tried to write down
everything we could remember.
For Claudia, this was not an easy
job, since she is the world's
worst speller and doesn't like to
write. She did it anyway, though,
which just goes to show what a
good friend she is.

Also, when we were back, safe
and sound, in good old Stoneybrook,
Connecticut, I interviewed my
friends. That was fun. Maybe I'll
be a reporter some day.

I haven't thought of a better
career.

Anyway, thanks to help from
members of the Baby-sitters Club--
Kristy Thomas, Jessi Ramsey,
Stacey McGill, Mallory Pike, Mary
Anne Spier (my best friend),
and Claudia, my co-disaster
victim, I managed to
write about the whole adventure,
even the parts that didn't
take place on the island.
In fact, even the parts that

took place in New York City, which, by the way, doesn't seem as exciting a place as a deserted island just now.

So... here goes my story.

-- Dawn Schafer

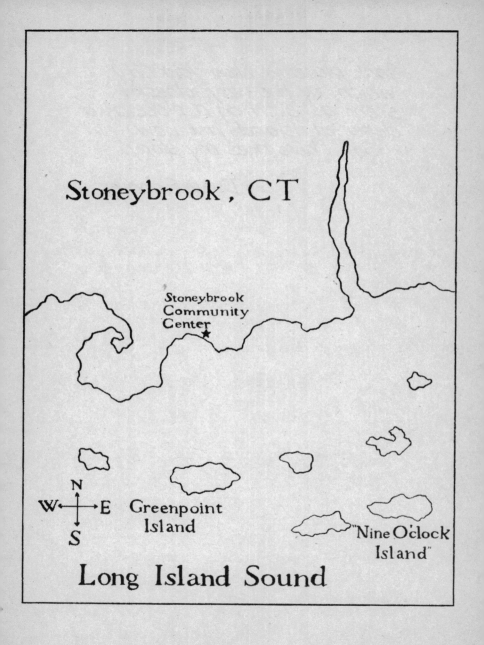

Stoneybrook, CT

Stoneybrook
Community
Center

Greenpoint
Island

"Nine O'clock
Island"

N
W E
S

Long Island Sound

Dawn

Looking Back - Friday
It all started with the
sailing lessons. Well, I guess if
I'm really going to be accurate,
I should say it all started
when Mallory Pike told me
that besides everything else
Stoneybrook's community
center offers (such as dance
classes, art lessons, and creative
theater), it also offers swimming
and boating classes, since the
center is located near the
water. Because I'm a good
swimmer (I've even passed a
life-saving test) and I like the
water and boats, I thought that
taking sailing lessons would be
fun. I'd been sailing before--pretty
many times, in fact. So had Claudia

Kishi. So we signed up for a sailing class at the community center. If we hadn't, we would never have been on our adventure.

"Well, are you ready?" I asked.

"Am I *ready*? I'm going to beat the pants off you!" replied Claudia.

We were on the phone, and we had challenged each other to a sailing race, which would be held the next day.

"No, you're not. I did tons of sailing with Dad and Jeff when I lived in California. And we go sailing almost every time I visit them now."

My parents are divorced. Mom and I live here in Stoneybrook, and Dad and Jeff live in California. Why? That's a long story. To make it short, let me just say that Mom grew up in Stoneybrook, but she met my father in California, where *he'd* grown up. After the divorce, it seemed natural for Mom to return to Connecticut with Jeff and me. But Jeff never adjusted to things here, so he went back to Dad and California, where he'd always been happy. I visit them whenever I can.

"Well, I sail every summer when we go away on vacation," said Claudia. "Face it. You and I are pretty evenly matched. We've been taking lessons from the same instructors for two months now."

"You're right. Tomorrow will be a close race. . . . But I'm still going to beat you!" I replied.

"I wish the instructors would let us race to Greenpoint without counselors along," said Claudia. "I don't want the counselors anymore." (Greenpoint is an island off the coast where the community center often holds special events.)

"I don't want the counselors, either. They're nice, but having them along is kind of a drag. It's like going clothes shopping with your parents."

"Besides, we've sailed to Greenpoint a million times." (That was an exaggeration, naturally.)

"I know," I said.

"I guess they're afraid we'll go off course. There *are* an awful lot of teeny, tiny islands all up and down the coast."

"Really?"

"Sure." (Claud knows Connecticut much better than I do, since she grew up here and I'm a recent transplant.) "Some of them are so small that people *own* them. Imagine owning an island. They look like pinpricks from up in an airplane. There must be hundreds of them." (This time, I knew Claud was not exaggerating.)

"Wow," I said.

"Anyway, get ready for Greenpoint," said Claud. "I'm going to bed now. I want to rest up for the big race."

Rest up. Ha! Claud just wanted a chance to go to bed early. She likes to get under the covers with a good Nancy Drew mystery. And, possibly, a candy bar.

I, on the other hand, was going to exercise, bulk up on some pasta, and get a normal amount of sleep. *That* was the way to win the race — wasn't it?

The next morning — Saturday — I woke up at seven-thirty. I exercised some more. Then I ate a healthy breakfast. I felt fit. I knew I was ready for the race. And I was pretty sure I could beat Claudia.

"You've got great racing weather," said Mary Anne.

Mary Anne is not just my best friend. She's my stepsister, too. My mom isn't single anymore. After we moved to Connecticut, Mom fell in love with — get this — her high-school sweetheart. He happened to be the father of the first friend I made in Stoneybrook — Mary Anne Spier. And not long ago, Mom and

Richard (that's Mary Anne's father, who was a widower) got married. Isn't that romantic? Then Richard, Mary Anne, and Tigger (Mary Anne's kitten) moved into our house.

"We have perfect weather," I said to Mary Anne. "Just perfect."

"Your mom and my dad and I are going to see you off," Mary Anne went on. "We'll be there for the finish, too. But I think I'll come home in between."

I could understand why. Mary Anne has super-sensitive skin. She gets as red as a lobster after about half an hour in the sun. No kidding. And Greenpoint Island, the place Claudia and I were going to race to and from, is almost three miles out in Long Island Sound. No way could Mary Anne stand around in the sun for a six-mile race.

"That's okay," I told her. As I mentioned before, Mary Anne and I understand each other.

Two hours later, Richard was driving our family to the community center.

"You know," said Mary Anne, "I really hope you win."

I almost replied, "Duh." Why *wouldn't* she want her own sister to win? But instead I just said, "Thanks."

"I wouldn't mind if Claud won, though," she went on.

"You *what?*"

(Richard glanced at us in the rearview mirror.)

"Well, it's just — you know." (Mary Anne lowered her voice.) "Claudia's report card." We get report cards several times a year.

"What about it?" I asked.

"It wasn't very good. I think she's feeling pretty bad about herself right now. If she won the race, she might feel better."

"That's true," I said slowly, thinking it over.

"At least her parents didn't make her drop out of the Baby-sitters Club," Mary Anne pointed out. (They're always threatening to do that. The BSC is a business that my friends and I run. We baby-sit for families in our neighborhoods.)

"Yeah."

We drove the rest of the way to the community center in silence. When we reached it, the first person I saw was Claudia, and did she ever look ready to race — and win.

"Good luck!" called Mom and Richard and Mary Anne. They joined a bunch of other people who were standing on the dock. Claudia's parents and sister were there, and so were the rest of our friends in the BSC, as well as Logan

Bruno, who is Mary Anne's steady boyfriend (and also an adjunct member of the club), plus a few interested kids and some people from the center.

The race started off well (for me) since I was ahead. I had dressed properly for sailing — loose, comfortable clothing that I could move around in, and that wouldn't get caught in anything. Claudia, on the other hand, couldn't help dressing up just a little. She is a real clotheshorse, and I guess she wanted to look good, since she knew we'd have an audience. So she'd put on a tank top and baggy drawstring pants. Over the top, she was wearing a button-down shirt of her father's. The sleeves were rolled up, but none of the buttons were buttoned. She was also wearing big earrings that she had made herself. Claudia is quite artistic. So the thing is, she *looked* good but, as it turned out, she was not dressed for sailing.

As soon as we were on the water and had picked up some speed, her shirt started blowing around. She was busier peeling the shirt off her face than she was steering the boat or doing anything else. *Then* one of her huge earrings got caught on a sail and she had to struggle to set it free. With the wind blowing around me, I couldn't hear anything from her

13

boat, but I could see her lips moving and I bet she was saying some things she isn't supposed to say. Anyway, the counselor took her earrings off for her, and Claudia buttoned up her shirt. Still, I reached Greenpoint before she did.

I lost no time turning round and heading back, but this time the wind had changed direction, and I had trouble steering.

Uh-oh, I thought. Claudia's going to catch up. Sure enough, the closer we got to the community center, the closer Claudia got to *me*. By the time the race was over . . .

"Tie! It's a tie!" yelled Kristy Thomas from her place in the crowd.

Everyone agreed with her. Personally, I thought I was about an inch ahead of Claud at the end, but who am I to argue with twenty people, most of whom are my friends?

The only good thing that came of the race was that the head sailing instructor said Claud and I didn't need counselors with us anymore. "No sailing *alone*," she cautioned, "but you don't need counselors."

"Thank you," said Claud and I politely, even though we both wanted to cheer.

Then Claudia challenged me to a rematch. Of course, I accepted. If only I'd known what would happen when we raced again.

CHAPTER 2

Mary Anne

Looking Back-
Monday

Ordinarily, I don't record what happens at a meeting of the Baby-sitters Club. I just make appointments for sitting jobs. But when Dawn decided she wanted to write about her adventure, I looked back at the record book to see if I could remember what had happened at that Monday BSC meeting before Claud and Dawn's rematch.

It was two days after the race, the race that Claudia almost lost due to

*earrings and bad dressing.
Kristy was trying to
conduct an official
meeting, but all my
stepsister and Claud
could talk about was
their race. Each thought
she had won....*

"It was just my earrings," complained Claud.

"And your shirt," Dawn couldn't help pointing out.

Claudia made a face. She is the vice-president of the Baby-sitters Club. Her job is . . . well, she's VP because she has her own phone and personal, private phone number, so her room is the perfect place to hold our Monday, Wednesday, and Friday club meetings.

What *is* the Baby-sitters Club? Well, it's really a business. It's a group of girls (the seven that Dawn mentioned) who get together three times a week and arrange sitting jobs. Our clients know we meet at these times because we do a lot of advertising. They call us during meetings to line up baby-sitters for their children.

Another reason Claud is the VP is that we invade her room three times a week. She pro-

vides us with snacks, if needed. Claudia is as addicted to junk food as she is to Nancy Drew books, but since her parents don't approve of either habit, she has to hide both the food and the books all over her room. Claud lives with her parents and her older sister, Janine, who is a true genius. Too bad for Claud. She loves her sister, but it's not easy living with a genius when you're a poor student, even if you are smart. I wished Claud had gotten a better report card. I almost wished she'd win the rematch. Then she would feel better about herself. Sometimes Claudia thinks she's not good at *anything* except art and baby-sitting.

"Can we please get back to the matter at hand?" asked Kristy, sounding agitated. (She meant the meeting.) Kristy is the president of the BSC, since it was her idea, and she's always getting lots of other ideas for keeping the club running — and running well. She tries to conduct the meetings in a businesslike manner, but that day she actually seemed cross. And I knew it wasn't because of us. Dawn is my best friend, and Kristy is my other best friend. I know her like the back of my hand. Something was wrong. Was it her family? Kristy lives in a big, mixed-up family with a stepfather, a stepbrother, a stepsister, an adopted sister, her grandmother, her mother and her brothers, not to mention two pets.

"Kristy?" I said tentatively. (I hate confrontations and I cry easily.) "Is anything wrong?"

"Oh . . ." Kristy sighed heavily. "I'm sorry. It's the Krushers." (The Krushers are the kids on a softball team that Kristy organized and coaches.) "They're upset. We lost to the Bashers *again*. The kids are getting a little discouraged. They think they'll never win a game. What they don't see is that they're getting better all the time. Maybe they'll win next Monday. We've got another game then."

We had a three-day weekend coming up, which we were all looking forward to as if we'd never had a vacation in our lives.

"Well, we'll come cheer the Krushers on," spoke up Stacey, our treasurer. It's her job to collect club dues and handle money; to make sure we have enough in the treasury to help Claud pay her monthly phone bill, for instance. Stacey is Claudia's best friend, and it's easy to see why. The two of them are chic, sophisticated, and trendy. Stacey grew up in New York City. (She's so lucky. As soon as I'm old enough, I plan to move there.) But now she lives in Stoneybrook. Her parents got divorced recently, and her father still lives in the Big Apple, so Stacey gets to go to the city and visit him any weekend she wants. Lately she hasn't been going in as often as usual, though. Stacey has diabetes and hasn't been feeling great. I think her visits have turned into command performances. Her father says, "Come," and Stacey goes, whether she wants to or not.

"Thanks, Stacey," said Kristy, and at that moment, the phone rang. "Oh, goody. A job call!" she went on, her eyes brightening.

"I'll get it," said Dawn. Dawn is our alternate officer, which means she's like a substitute teacher. She knows what's involved in being any officer of the club, and can handle that job if one of us has to miss a meeting. That doesn't give her much to do most of the time, though, so since Dawn likes to be busy, she answers the phone a lot.

"Hello, Baby-sitters Club," she said.

I got out the record book. I'm the club secretary and it's my duty to arrange sitting jobs, and also to know everybody's schedule — when Kristy has a Krushers' practice or Mallory has an orthodontist appointment or Jessi has a ballet class.

"Tuesday afternoon?" Dawn was saying. "I'll get right back to you, Mrs. Prezzioso."

"Uh-oh," I said, as Dawn hung up and everyone else began groaning — and hoping they were busy on Tuesday.

Jenny Prezzioso is a brat. (I'm sorry, but she is.) I'm really the only one who can tolerate her. Unfortunately, I wasn't free on Tuesday. But Mallory was. "It's your job," I told her.

"Swell," replied Mal sarcastically.

"Hey, junior officer," said Kristy. "That's what you're here for."

"I know, I know."

Mallory Pike and Jessi Ramsey are our junior officers because they're younger than the rest of us. They're eleven and in sixth grade, while we're thirteen and in eighth grade. (By the way, we all attend Stoneybrook Middle School, or SMS.) Mal and Jessi joined the club to give us a hand with afternoon jobs, since they're not allowed to baby-sit at night unless they're sitting for their own families.

Although Mal and Jessi come from different backgrounds and have very different families, they're best friends — and they do have some things in common. Here are the differences: Mallory is white, has *seven* younger brothers and sisters, wants to be a children's book author, and grew up in Stoneybrook. Jessi is black, has just one younger sister and a baby brother, is a talented dancer, and recently moved to Connecticut from New Jersey. Here are the similarities: Both Mal and Jessi like to

21

read, especially horse stories, and both feel that their parents treat them like babies. However, their parents are loosening up a little. They allowed their daughters to get their ears pierced, Mal's parents let her get a new haircut, and — get this — Jessi's parents were letting her sit for Becca and Squirt (her sister and brother) all by herself for the entire upcoming long weekend. What a breakthrough.

Mallory reluctantly agreed to sit for Jenny Prezzioso on Tuesday. When that was arranged and the phone didn't ring for awhile, Claudia brought up the rematch again. It was sort of an obsession with her.

"How about this Saturday?" she suggested. "This time *I am* going to win. What a way to start off the weekend."

"This Saturday," Dawn repeated slowly. "I don't know. Jeff's going to be visiting. The kid gets a *four*-day weekend at *his* school. I don't want to miss being — Hey, wait! Maybe Jeff could come *with* me! We don't need counselors anymore, but we're not allowed to sail alone."

"Well, then, *I've* got to get a crew member, too," said Claud. She looked at Mal. "How about it?"

I knew she was choosing Mallory because, except for her sister Margo, who gets seasick, the Pike family loves boating and they spend a lot of time on the water.

"I'd like to," Mal replied, looking flattered, "but Mom and Dad have activities planned for the weekend."

Jessi spoke up shyly. "I think Becca would *die* to go with you," she said. "She's hardly ever been on a boat, but she'd think it was really exciting. She's — she's been a little jealous recently because of my dancing. She'd like to find something athletic — and different — that *she* could be good at. What do you think? She learns quickly."

"I think I'd love to have Becca along," Claud answered.

So Dawn called her mother to get permission to hold the rematch on Saturday and to ask if Jeff could sail with her. Then Jessi called her parents and, even though they were frantically making last-minute plans for their weekend away, they said that Becca could go sailing with Claudia.

It was settled. My friends were going to hold their rematch on Saturday — and they had found crew members.

CHAPTER 3

Dawn

Looking Back—Tuesday and Wednesday

By the next day, the day after our meeting, the rematch had turned into more than just another race. It was to be an outing as well. All it took was a few phone calls -- to Jeff, who was still in California, to Becca, to Mr. and Mrs. Newton, and to Mr. and Mrs. Braddock.

"What a great day Saturday is going to be!" exclaimed Claudia.

As it turned out, she was half right. It started out as a great day, but the ending was... well, you'll see.

On Monday, Mom had approved of Jeff as my crew member, but I thought I better clear it with him personally. What if he arrived on Friday and didn't want to go sailing for some reason? Then I'd have to scramble around for a new crew member. And if I couldn't find one, then we'd have to reschedule the match, and Becca would be disappointed, and Claud would be upset. I wasn't really worrying. I was just examining all angles.

I was looking at the big picture.

So on Monday night, I called Jeff. The three-hour time difference between the East Coast and the West Coast is such a pain. I usually wait until ten o'clock P.M. my time, knowing Jeff and Dad will probably be home at seven o'clock their time. I also usually interrupt their dinner.

Tuesday was no exception.

At ten on the nose, I picked up the phone and dialed my dad's house. Jeff answered. (He loves to answer the phone.) Usually, he answers it normally, but that night he said in a deep voice, "Hello, Marcel's Dry Cleaning."

I knew it was Jeff right away, and began giggling.

"Hey, dweeb," I said affectionately. "You can't fool me. This is your sister."

"Hey, geek."

"Who were you expecting? A friend of yours?"

Jeff lowered his voice. "No, Carol." (Carol is Dad's girlfriend. Jeff and I don't like her much, although I think she's growing on Jeff. But he still tries to cut her off from Dad sometimes.)

"Jeff! That's not nice."

"I know," he replied.

I couldn't help laughing.

"Do you want to talk to Dad?" asked my brother.

"Maybe in a few minutes. I want to talk to you first, though. It's about this weekend."

"Oh, no! It's off, isn't it? You guys decided to go away or something, didn't you?"

"Of course not, dweeb. Claudia and I are having a sailing race on Saturday and I want to know if you'd like to be my crew member. We're sailing to Greenpoint Island and back." (Jeff had been there once before.) "Mom already said you could go," I added.

"Really? Awesome! I'm there!"

"Terrific!"

I talked to Jeff a few minutes longer, and then to Dad, but Dad and I were interrupted when Carol dropped by.

Jeff got back on the phone. "The Hair Queen is here," he whispered.

I laughed again. Jeff's new nickname for Carol is the Hair Queen because she is constantly getting her hair cut or dyed or something.

When Jeff and I hung up, I called Claud right away.

"Hi," she said.

"Hi," I replied. "Well, Jeff's ready. He's really excited about the race."

"Great," said Claud, "but we've got one teeny-tiny problem."

"What?"

"Becca is so excited about the race that she started calling all her friends to tell them about it. Most of the kids just thought the race was neat, but Haley Braddock wants to come *with* us."

The Braddocks are clients of the BSC. They have two children — Haley, who's nine, and Matt, who's seven. Matt is profoundly deaf. That means that he really can't hear anything. And he has no speech. He goes to a school for the deaf in Stamford, and he communicates using sign language. All the Braddocks use sign language, even Haley. In fact, she's almost an expert. So she's a neat kid, but I think sometimes she feels that Matt gets all the attention in her family. That was probably why she wanted to go boating so badly. It would be something special for *her*.

"Well, that is a problem," I agreed. "I'd hate to tell Haley she can't come with us when she wants an invitation so badly."

"I know . . ." replied Claud slowly. "But it's not fair for me to have two crew members and you to have only one, even though the kids won't be doing much. In fact, having Becca and Haley along might even make me *lose*. They're both pretty inexperienced."

"How about this?" I suggested brightly. "You let Haley come along, and I'll find a second crew member, too. One who's completely inexperienced, to make up for Jeff."

"Well. . . . Who would you ask?"

I thought for a few moments. At last I said, "I know this will sound crazy, but how about Jamie?"

"Jamie *Newton?*" cried Claud. "He's only four."

"I know, but he'd love this. He's a good swimmer — he's been taking lessons — and he has this thing for boats right now. They fascinate him. Can you imagine if he got to go on a sailing race?"

"He'd be in heaven," said Claud.

"The only thing," I went on, "is that he'd probably rather go in your boat than in mine." (Claudia and Jamie are very close.) "Do you think the girls would mind splitting up? Becca or Haley would have to go with you and Jamie then, and the other could come with Jeff and me. I'm positive Jeff will want to be in my boat. We'd still be pretty balanced in terms of our crew members."

"Listen, before we get carried away with details," said Claud, "we better call the Braddocks and the Newtons and get their permission. For all we know, they might be going away this weekend."

But they weren't. The adults were delighted with the invitations for Haley and Jamie, as long as we promised all the safety stuff, like making them wear life vests. We promised.

And on Wednesday, *another* dimension was added to our race. It was my idea. "Claud," I said to her in the school cafeteria that day, "instead of just racing to Greenpoint and back, how about making this a real outing for Jeff and the kids?"

"What kind of outing?" asked Claud.

"Well, we could race just *to* Greenpoint, not to Greenpoint and back. We could pack picnic lunches, and after the race, we could stay on the island for an hour or two, eat, let the kids

29

play in the water and look for shells and stuff, and then we could have a leisurely sail back home. That way, we'd still get our race in, and the kids could have some fun."

"I think that's a great idea!" exclaimed Claud. "We'll just have to get the parents' permission, that's all."

We took care of everything that afternoon. We talked to the Newtons and to my mom, to the Braddocks and to Jessi. Her parents weren't home, but she was sure they'd approve the outing since they'd already approved the race. Becca and Haley even said they wouldn't mind going in different boats.

We were set to sail!

CHAPTER 4

Dawn

Looking Back-Friday

I think that if I hadn't been so determined to win the race, I would never have had the fight with Mary Anne, and then what happened on the island wouldn't have seemed quite so bad. But we did have a fight and it was basically my fault. I say basically because, as Mary Anne's father always points out, "It takes two to tango." By that he means you can't have a one-sided fight. Mary Anne -- and Logan-- were part of the problem, too. But when you get right down to it, it was my fault....

Up, down. Up, down. Up, down. Puff, puff, puff, puff.

I was on a towel on the floor in the den, working out along with one of those exercise videos. The woman on the video seemed to have boundless energy, and I was proud to say that I did, too.

It was Friday afternoon, the day before the rematch. I had been working out all week. And I'd been bulking up on healthy, high-energy food. Of course, I didn't tell Claudia that. I was pretty sure she was sticking to her junk-food regimen and not exercising at all. She rarely does. Exercise, that is.

"All right!" said the video woman brightly. She bounced to her feet from a sitting position. How did she do that? Every time I reached that point in the tape I fell over. When I righted myself, I had to stop the tape, back it up, and start at the place where I'd tipped over sideways and gotten behind the instructions.

"And *one*, and *two*, and *three*, and *four*," said the instructor, sounding as if she belonged on *Sesame Street*. "*Lift* those legs. *Lift* those legs. Higher! Higher! *You* can *do* it!"

She sounded sort of silly, but the funny thing was, I found that if I tried, I *could* do it.

I lifted my legs higher than the day before.

The video woman started running in place. I ran in place with her. We were running to "Give My Regards to Broadway," which made us run pretty fast. I have to admit, I was relieved when the phone rang. I was the only one at home, so I would have to pause the tape to take the call.

Click. The video woman froze in running formation.

"I'll be right back," I told her.

I grabbed a small towel from the arm of a chair and patted myself off as I made a dash for the phone. I was all sweaty and out of breath.

"Hello?" I said, panting, as I picked up the receiver.

"Dawn? Is that you?" It was Logan Bruno, Mary Anne's boyfriend.

"Yeah," I gasped.

"Where'd I get you from?"

"Exercising." Pant, pant, pant.

"Oh. Sorry. Listen, is Mary Anne there?"

"No, she's sitting at the Perkinses' for a little while."

"Okay. Well, I've got a problem. Mary Anne and I were supposed to meet at the library around four-thirty — right after she finished at the Perkinses', I guess. But Hunter just had an asthma attack and Mom has taken him to the doctor, so I've got to stay here with Kerry until they get back, and I don't know when that will be."

Logan's little brother, Hunter, is allergic to everything in the world, and sometimes gets asthma attacks, which can be scary. Kerry is Logan's younger sister. It was lucky that Logan was at home to take care of her.

"Wow. I'm really sorry, Logan. I'll call Mary Anne at the Perkinses' for you and tell her what happened. I hope Hunter's okay."

"Thanks, Dawn."

We hung up and I was about to call Mary Anne when the phone rang again. This time it was Mom.

"Hi, sweetie," she said. "I'm just calling to tell you that I spoke to Richard a few minutes ago and we've decided to go out for an early dinner tonight. We thought it would be a nice way to start the weekend."

"Oh, great, Mom. Have fun!"

"Thanks. You and Mary Anne will be okay, won't you? If you don't see anything in the fridge you like, then go ahead and order in Chinese food or something."

"All *right!* Thank you." I wasn't sure if Chinese food was healthy, bulking-up stuff, but it sure sounded good. I was looking around the kitchen for our Chinese menus when I heard the video go on in the den again. The "pause" was over. I ran to the den, began the workout again, and had gotten as far as two running steps when the phone rang for a third time.

"*Darn!*" I exclaimed. I paused the tape and dashed back to the kitchen.

"Hello?" I said, picking up the phone.

"Hi, Sunshine. It's your old dad."

"Hi, Old Dad!"

"I just wanted to let you know that Jeff's safely on his way."

"Okay. We'll be picking him up late tonight. Mom and Richard are going out to dinner, but we'll all be at the airport in plenty of time to meet Jeff. I can't wait to see him."

"Well, have a great weekend. Jeff told me about the race. Good luck! I know you'll win."

When Dad and I got off the phone, I hung around in the kitchen, waiting for the phone to ring again. When it didn't, I *finally* returned to my workout and was able to keep at it without interruptions. I planned to exercise until almost five o'clock (if I could stand it), then quickly shower and change my clothes. That would give me just enough time to get to the Friday BSC meeting.

"And *one*, and *two* . . ."

I managed to exercise until 4:45. Then I had to stop. My muscles felt as if they were coiled springs — too tight. I cooled down for awhile, went upstairs, peeled off my sweaty workout clothes, and stepped into the shower.

Ahhhh. I stood there forever, just letting the hot water spray my back. Finally I had to turn off the water, though. If I didn't, I wouldn't be dried off and dressed in time to make the meeting.

It was just as I was slipping a shirt on over my head that I heard our front door open and then close with a bang.

"Mary Anne?" I called. "Is that you?"

"Yes," she answered shortly. She sounded pretty mad.

The next sound I heard was footsteps pounding up the stairs and into Mom and Richard's room.

"Hey, Sis," I said. "Is something the matter?"

"Yes, something is the matter. Logan stood me up, that's what."

By that time I was leaning against the doorway to our parents' room. Mary Anne was sitting in a chair, dialing the phone.

Uh-oh, I thought. I didn't call the Perkinses' to give Logan's message to Mary Anne.

"Um, Mary Anne," I began.

But Mary Anne was already saying, "Logan?" and waving her hand at me to be quiet.

From then on I could only hear Mary Anne's end of the conversation, of course, but from the things she said I had a pretty good idea of what went on. And I have rarely seen Mary Anne so mad.

"Logan! What are you doing at home? Have you been there all afternoon? We were supposed to meet at the library at four-thirty. Where were you? You stood me up!"

Logan must have said something like, "I did *not* stand you up," because Mary Anne said, "Well, you weren't there. I waited and waited."

"Mary *Anne!*" I hissed.

Mary Anne put her hand over the receiver and said, "SHHH! Logan and I are *trying* to have an argument. Would you please leave me alone?"

I stopped leaning against the doorjamb, but I just edged out into the hallway where I could hear the rest of the conversation. I knew Logan and Mary Anne would figure out what I'd done and that I'd be in trouble pretty soon. I wanted to be prepared for it.

The next thing I heard Mary Anne say was,

"How could you stand me up? Did you just forget? Or did you have something better to do?"

Logan must have said he had something better to do and then told her about Hunter's asthma attack and his call to me. Because soon Mary Anne was saying, "Well, Dawn never called me," and "Logan, I'm so sorry."

But apparently Logan wasn't accepting Mary Anne's apology. I guess he just couldn't believe that Mary Anne would think he'd stand her up. Mary Anne kept saying, "I'm sor — Logan, I'm really — Logan, I'm sorry. I — " But Logan wouldn't let her get a word in edgewise. Which of course made Mary Anne madder than ever at Logan.

Finally, she hung up on him!

Whoa, I thought, as I fled to my room. (I didn't want Mary Anne to know I'd been eavesdropping.) When Mary Anne appeared at the door to my room (which took all of about two seconds), she just stood there and glared at me.

Before she could say a word, I blurted out, "I'm sorry, I'm sorry, I'm sorry. Logan gave me the message for you and I was going to call you right away, but before I could, Mom called, and then Dad called, and I guess — I guess I just forgot . . . I *meant* to tell you."

"But you didn't."

I changed the subject. "I've never heard you hang up on Logan before."

"Were you *eaves*dropping?" Mary Anne's voice was growing shrill.

I looked at my watch. "Uh-oh. If we don't hustle, we're going to be late for the meeting." I took off down the stairs.

Mary Anne followed, but she didn't let up on me. We argued the entire time we were riding our bicycles over to Claud's house, the BSC headquarters.

"Didn't you *tell* Logan I forgot to give you the message?" I asked as we pedaled toward Bradford Court.

"Of course I did," she snapped. "But he's mad at me for thinking that he'd stand me up."

I sighed. Logan and Mary Anne are usually so understanding of each other. This fight was unlike them. So I felt terrible. Because of me, Logan and Mary Anne were *very* mad at each other. And Mary Anne was furious with me. So furious, in fact, that as we parked our bikes on the Kishis' driveway, she said, "You know what? I wish I never had to see you again. I wish you would get out of my life — forever."

CHAPTER 5

Claudia

Looking Back —
Satruday mornig and afternn

Uh oh. Dawn and Mary Ann are not speaking
to each other. I fell bad for Dawn on the
other hand mabe if she ~~cant cousin cke~~ keep
her mind on the race Ill win but then it
woldnt realy be fiar.

I tired not to think of my friends figt. I
tired to think of the race and the picknick
insted. I packed a baskit full of food I tired
to pack stuff that wold be hethy for the kids
but I couldnt help paking a lot of candy bares to.

Saturday was another perfect day for sailing. I woke up to a clear blue sky with some puffy white clouds and just enough of a breeze to make our sailing race fun and challenging.

That morning I dressed sensibly for our rematch. No jewelry at all (I was not about to lose on account of earrings), and a long-sleeved jersey that I could tuck into my jeans. I even pulled my hair back and braided it so it wouldn't blow in my face.

At about ten o'clock my phone rang. I was just finishing putting on my makeup. (I didn't see how I could possibly lose a race on account of *makeup*.) I screwed the mascara tube together and picked up the receiver.

"Hello?" I said. (Sometimes I forget and say, "Hello, Baby-sitters Club," even when we aren't having a meeting.)

"Hi, it's me." Dawn. My friends and I know each other so well, we don't even have to say who's calling.

"Are you chickening out?" I asked immediately.

"No!"

"Oh. What's up?"

"I was calling to see if you were chickening out."

"No! I'm ready to go. I'm going to cream you."

"We'll see."

"Are you and Mary Anne speaking to each other?" I asked.

There was a pause. Finally Dawn said, "Not exactly." Then she changed her mind and said, "Not at all."

I wasn't sure how to respond to that. Luckily, Dawn didn't seem to need a response. She went on talking. "What, um, what are you wearing?" she asked. I could tell she was trying not to laugh.

"Jeans, a polo shirt, sneakers, and a visor. And my hair is braided, and I do not have any jewelry on," I answered indignantly.

"I'm just teasing you," Dawn said. "Listen, I've packed granola bars, all-natural peanut butter sandwiches, bananas, some salad made without mayonnaise — you know, so it won't go bad — some yogurt, a few juice boxes, and a lot of bottled spring water for Jeff and me. We love spring water. What are you putting in your picnic basket?" she asked.

"Bologna sandwiches, apples, a big bottle of Coke, and fifteen candy bars. Do you think we have enough food?"

"For an army," said Dawn. "Okay. I'll see

you at the community center at eleven o'clock. Be there or be square."

I giggled. Then we hung up our phones.

An hour later, a crowd of people was at the boat dock. There were my parents, my sister, and me; Dawn, her mother, and her stepfather; Jessi, Becca, and Squirt (who'd been driven over by Haley and her family, who were also there); Jamie, his parents, and his baby sister; Kristy; Stacey; Mallory, her father, and two of her brothers, who were all going to go sailing themselves later; and a few counselors.

Mary Anne and Logan were not there. That was because Logan was mad at Mary Anne, and Mary Anne was mad at Dawn.

Dawn and I had each chosen a boat for the race. We had stowed our picnic baskets in them, made sure each boat had a first-aid kit and three life preservers, and now we were coating ourselves and the kids with sunscreen.

While this was going on — in fact, while I was rubbing sunscreen on every part of Jamie's body that wasn't covered up — he and his mother were having this conversation:

"Honey, I just don't know if you should go."

"But I feel fine, Mommy."

"But you had the sniffles yesterday."

"I *still* feel fine."

"I don't know . . ."

"Puh-*lease?* Please, please, please? Pretty please with a cherry on top? I promise I'll never bother Lucy again." (Lucy is Jamie's sister.) "And I'll do whatever you tell me from now on. I'll clean up my room, and I won't leave my sneakers on the stairs — "

"Okay, okay, okay." Mrs. Newton gave in. Almost. "Are you *sure* you feel okay?"

"I . . . FEEL . . . *FINE!*"

"OKAY!"

Jamie and his mother were laughing by then.

I jumped into the conversation. "I promise I'll make Jamie wear his windbreaker the whole day," I told Mrs. Newton. "That way he won't get cold. And he'll have to wear shoes on the boat, so don't worry about cold feet. And if anything seems wrong, we'll just turn around and come back, okay?"

Mrs. Newton smiled. "All right. I guess I'm just a little nervous. The last time Jamie had the sniffles, it turned into walking pneumonia."

Walking pneumonia? What was that? Anyway, Jamie looked fine to me. He wasn't even sniffling.

"Okay!" shouted Dawn from behind me. "Who's ready to go sailing?"

"I am!" cried Jamie, Jeff, Haley, and Becca.

The kids followed us to our boats. Dawn and I strapped life preservers on the children. Then we strapped life preservers on ourselves. We always wear them. Anything could happen, and smack — you'd find yourself in the ocean. Even the best swimmer needs to be prepared.

When the kids were ready, Dawn suddenly became very official.

"Life preservers?" she asked.

"Check," I replied, without bothering to look, since we had *just* strapped everybody in and the counselors had helped us.

"Food?"

"Check."

"First-aid kits?"

"Check."

"Let's go!"

Then Jamie, Haley, and Becca turned nervous on us. They ran back to their families for extra hugs. For just a moment, I thought the Newtons were going to convince Jamie to stay at home. But they didn't. A few minutes later,

Jamie, Becca, and I were settled in one boat, and Dawn, Jeff, and Haley were in another.

A counselor was poised on the dock. "Get ready!" he shouted. "Get set, and . . . GO!" He lowered his arm like he was starting a car race.

I almost giggled, but I knew I had to concentrate on the rematch.

We were off. Behind us I could hear people calling things like, "Good-bye!" and, "Have fun!" and, "See you later!" and, "Wear your windbreaker!" (Guess who said that.)

As we sailed along, we picked up speed. I love the feeling of wind. I think that's why I like to ski, too. I was glad I had tied my hair back, though.

I focused and concentrated. We could see Greenpoint Island, so we knew where we were going. I felt strong. I felt powerful.

"Claudia?" said Becca after a little while.

"What?" I replied.

"This is so, so cool." I could hardly hear Becca, but it wasn't just because of the wind rushing by. She was speaking quietly, like she was in a church or something. And I knew why. We were out on the water, away from the edge of our country. If we just kept going and going we would hit . . . I wasn't sure what. I used to think it was England, but Ja-

nine the Genius told me I was wrong. Anyway, there was nothing but air above us and water below us. And land, but that was way off in the distance. It was, as Becca had said, so, so cool.

For awhile, my boat was ahead. Although I listened to Becca, and kept a careful eye on her and Jamie, I was doing my best sailing.

"Hey, you guys!" yelled Jamie to Dawn's boat, which wasn't far behind. "We're going to win this race. We're going to beat you."

I wasn't sure whether Dawn and Jeff and Haley could hear Jamie until Haley yelled back, "Are not!"

"Are too!" said Becca.

"Are not!"

"Are too!"

After awhile, Dawn's boat caught up with ours. She grinned at me. I gritted my teeth. The are-not, are-tooing went on — until Dawn pulled ahead. Then Haley, to throw Becca off the track, yelled, "Are too!"

And Becca found herself calling, "Are not!"

When we realized what she'd said, we all began to laugh.

And that was how we spent the next hour or so. First one boat was ahead, then another. The kids yelled things to each other and giggled constantly. Jamie claimed he was starving, so he ate a peanut butter sandwich. Then Becca said *she* was starving and ate an apple and a candy bar.

"Hey, save some room and some food for the pic — " I started to say.

But I was interrupted by a shout from Dawn. "Claudia, look!" she cried. She was pointing to the sky.

I looked up. Huge thunderheads were forming. A chill ran through my body, even though the sun was still shining brightly. A storm was brewing, and Dawn and I both knew that out here — on this beautiful water — a storm could become a squall and sneak up on you quickly.

And be really nasty.

"Dawn!" I yelled, our race already forgotten. "We better decide what to do — and fast."

Dawn

Looking back –
Saturday afternoon

Claud and I knew we were in trouble the second we saw those clouds. Well, I knew, anyway, and I'm pretty sure from the look on Claud's face that she knew, too. I think even Jeff did. But Becca, Haley, and Jamie didn't look nervous until the storm actually hit. And I have to give them credit for this: All three of them kept their heads, especially the girls. Jamie cried a little, but what else would you expect from a four-year-old? I tried hard not to think about lost boats and shipwrecks....

The clouds piled up until they looked like mountains in the sky, and a haze formed quickly. None of this took as long as you might think. In fact, it happened more quickly than Claud or I would have expected. Soon, I knew, the sky would be a mass of dark clouds.

I steered my boat as close to Claudia's as I could, which wasn't easy, considering the wind that was blowing up.

"Claud!" I shouted. I had to yell loudly in order for her to hear me.

"Yeah?"

"We better turn back."

"No!" Claudia shook her head. "I know we can't see it anymore, but we're closer to Greenpoint now than we are to the shore. If we keep going ahead, we might reach the island. If we turn around, we probably won't . . . you know." Claudia glanced at Jamie and Becca. She was trying not to scare them.

Even though Claudia had grown up here and knew Greenpoint and this area much better than I did, I shouted back to her, "Are you *sure* we shouldn't turn around?"

"Positive!"

So we kept moving ahead. Sailing was becoming a struggle. I told Jeff what we were up against because I knew he could handle it,

51

and would then be a help. He tightened the straps on our life vests and made Haley sit down out of the way. Then he secured anything that might blow away.

Claudia didn't have such help. She was on her own in her boat, holding the sail, trying to steer, checking life vests, doing everything herself.

As the wind blew even harder and the first raindrops began to fall, I noticed that Claudia's boat was ahead of mine.

"Hurray!" yelled Jamie, obviously unaware of trouble.

But I yelled, "Claud, let the sail out — we have to stay together! We can't let ourselves get separated."

"I'm trying to stay with you," she called back, and I could barely hear her. "But the wind is awfully strong."

So were the waves. The water was growing choppier by the second. Our boat was tossed fiercely by the ocean. Sometimes a wave would slap right over our boat. Other times we were bounced in the air.

"It's just like a water ride at the amusement park!" said Haley gleefully as Jeff rushed around, covering things with sheets of plastic. I was extremely glad he was there.

The sky, by that time, had grown so dark

that it looked almost like night. I could barely see Claud's boat.

"Claudia?" I shouted.

"Don't worry. I'm here!"

Okay. She was over to our right.

And then, without warning, that black, black sky just opened up. It was as if it were so full of rain that it couldn't hold it in any longer. And the only way to lighten up was to dump all the water on us.

Which it did.

The rain came down in sheets. Now Jeff tried to cover himself and Haley and me with the plastic, but it didn't do any good. The wind blew it off of us, and the plastic was whisked away into the darkness.

"Dawn? Dawn?" Claudia was calling to me.

"I'm here. I'm still to your left!" I yelled.

If only we could see each other, I thought. And then I *could* see Claud — but just her face. It was lit up against the storm.

"Your flashlight!" she called. "You've got a flashlight under the seat next to the first-aid kit."

Jeff found it and turned it on. It didn't light our way (it wasn't strong enough), but at least Claud and I could keep track of each other.

It was at this point, with the choppy water, the sheets of rain, and the gusty wind, that

Haley said to me, "Dawn? I don't want to be rude or anything, but I'm not having fun anymore."

"Well, we're in a little trouble," I told Haley. "This is a bad storm. We're trying to reach Greenpoint Island but I'm not sure we're on course. The best thing to do is just hold on tight. And if I give you any instructions, follow them. No questions asked, okay?"

"Okay," replied Haley shakily.

In Claud's boat, Becca grew nervous faster than Haley did, and Jamie began to cry. He cried hard at first, but soon he was just sniffling. Everybody held together as well as they could.

And then it happened.

A *huge* wave washed over our boat. Haley was thrown off her seat by the force of it. Remembering my instructions to "hold on tight," she grabbed for the nearest object — which happened to be the rudder. The rudder snapped and Haley went flying again. This time *I* made a grab for *her*. I caught her life vest.

Haley was safe.

But from the other end of the boat Jeff was screaming, "Dawn! The boat's full of water!"

"Well, that was a big wave," I pointed out.

"No, it's not just that. There's water coming

in from somewhere else!" Jeff was frantically trying to rescue our supplies while I settled Haley on a seat again. I noticed that she was in water halfway up to her knees. Whoa. This was serious.

"Hey! You guys!" yelled Claudia. "Stay with us! You keep drifting away!"

"Our rudder's broken!" I shouted. "And our boat's filling up with water."

It was at that point, as I noticed Claudia's flashlight bobbing away, that Jeff, trying not to sound frightened, crossed the boat and tried to whisper to me (which was not easy), "We're sinking."

"We're what?" I'd heard him, but I didn't want to believe him.

"We're sinking," he repeated quietly.

I looked at Haley. The water was creeping closer to her knees.

"I guess we're going to have to bail out," I told him. "We'll try to get Claud to steer as close to us as she can — "

"Then I'll toss our supplies to her," Jeff interrupted.

"Oh, good thinking," I said, "and then we'll have to . . . just hold onto her boat and float, I guess. We can't get into the boat. We'll be too heavy. I'll help you and Haley, since I passed the life-saving test."

"Okay." No arguments from Jeff.

"Claud!" I yelled again.

"What?"

"We're going to have to bail out and swim to your boat. There's nothing else to do. We're sinking."

"Okay," replied Claud tightly. I could tell she was nervous. Six people and one small sailboat was not a good idea. There would be too much weight. But what choice did we have?

"Can you steer over here?" I yelled. My teeth were chattering. The ocean and the rain were cold.

"I'll try."

The flashlight on Claud's boat bobbed closer to ours. Soon I could actually make out Claudia, Jamie, and Becca. They looked terrified — and as cold as I felt.

"First," I yelled to Claud, "Jeff's going to toss our supplies to you. We better hang onto everything we can."

"Okay!" Claud replied, and she and Becca caught the things as Jeff threw them. They tried to stow them under the seats or in plastic.

"All right, now we're going to swim to your boat," I said, trying to stay calm. At that point, it didn't look difficult. Claudia was right next to us. I thought we could reach her without much swimming — but immediately a huge wave separated us.

"Okay, you first, Haley," I said, climbing overboard. "I'll help you."

"I don't *want* to go in the water!" she cried.

"I'm sorry, but you have to. I'll swim you to Claudia and she and Becca will help you hang onto their boat. There's no room for us *in* the boat. Remember, you've got your life vest on, so you can't sink."

Haley looked at our boat. She saw that water was now rapidly filling it.

"Okay, here goes," she said bravely. She held her nose (which was unnecessary because of the life vest) and jumped overboard. Just in time I found her hand and swam with her. I didn't want us separated.

The distance to Claudia's boat, thankfully, wasn't too far, and Haley dogpaddled to it fairly quickly, with just a little help from me. Claudia and Becca pulled her to the side, and Becca grabbed her wrists.

Then, wordlessly, I turned around and headed back for Jeff. He was poised to jump in — and leave our boat behind.

"Go ahead!" I yelled to Jeff.

Splash! I caught Jeff as he jumped in. Then,

hand-in-hand, we swam to Claudia's boat. He and I clung to the sides without help. We were on our own.

"Claud?" I shouted. "Are we still on course?"

"I have no idea," she replied. "It's been so windy. But — Hey, wait! I see land ahead! Honest! Maybe it's Greenpoint!"

"Hurray!" cheered Jamie, through chattering teeth.

In just a few minutes, I could feel sand under my feet. We really had reached land. We walked the boat ashore and unloaded the supplies. The rain was letting up. The sky was brightening.

"Come on, you guys, we have to find shelter and dry off," said Claud, taking charge.

I was glad to let her do so. I didn't feel up to it.

So Jeff, Haley, and Becca began unloading our things from the boat. While they were busy, Claudia turned to me. "You know what?" she said.

"What?" I replied.

"This isn't Greenpoint Island. I don't know where we are."

I felt like crying.

CHAPTER 7

Jessi

Looking Back
Saturday

Oh, what a day. This has to have been the worst of my life. It started out okay, I guess. Well, Mama and Daddy left for their trip, and Becca immediately burst into tears. Like she hasn't stayed alone with me before. Squirt didn't know what was going on, so he was no problem.

Becca brightened, though, when she thought of her special sailboat outing. And by the time she'd

59

Jessi

*put on her bathing
suit, a T-shirt, a
pair of shorts, and
her sneakers, she
couldn't wait for the
Braddocks to pick us
up and take us to
the dock.*

*Once she was gone,
I spent a pleasant
day with Squirt —
until the thunderstorm.
That put an end to
the pleasantness....*

As you can see, I've started keeping a journal. Mallory made me do it. She's been keeping journals for ages, and has several notebooks full of her thoughts and feelings. I have to admit that I like keeping a journal. I don't write in it every night — just whenever I feel like it. But I wrote in it a lot while Becca was gone. That turned out to be pretty handy for Dawn, who needed things like journal entries in order to put together the whole story of her adventure.

Anyway, Squirt and I, as I mentioned, spent a very nice day together. He's at a really fun age — but a tiring one, too. He not only walks, but he runs (sort of) and he's still a mean crawler. By the time he went down for his afternoon nap on Saturday, I was exhausted. (How does my mother do it, all day, every day?) I was hoping to make myself a nice glass of iced tea, put my feet up, and lose myself in *Stormy, Misty's Foal*, which I have read only about a zillion times. But I had gotten two pages further into the book when — *BAM!*

Thunder.

Squirt was awake instantly. That was the end of his nap and my nice rest period.

Squirt hates thunder. He kept putting his hands over his ears and crying big alligator tears.

"Shh, shh," I said softly. "It'll be over soon. And then Becca will come back and we'll have hot dogs for dinner. How's that?"

Well, things did not go exactly as I'd planned. In fact, they went as far as possible in the other direction.

At five o'clock (the thunderstorm over), I said brightly to Squirt, "Becca will be home any minute now!"

At five-thirty, I said to him, "I wonder where your sister is. I'm getting hungry for hot dogs and I bet you are, too."

At six, I said, sounding out-and-out worried, "Where on earth is Becca? She should have been home by now. If she's playing at Haley's and didn't tell me, she's in for it."

I called the Braddocks.

"Hi, Mr. Braddock," I began. And just as I said, "Is Becca at your house playing with Haley?" *he* said, "Is Haley at your house playing with Becca?"

Then we both said, "No," at the same time.

"I don't think they're back yet," said Mr. Braddock, and I knew he meant Claudia, Dawn, and their sailing crews.

"But they should be back by now!" I cried.

I wanted to believe that they really were back, so I called Mary Anne next. "Dawn's back, isn't she?" I asked her nervously.

"I don't know and I don't care," replied Mary Anne haughtily.

"Come on," I said. "This is important. Is she back?"

"No," said Mary Anne.

I called the Kishis and the Newtons next, knowing full well that they would say that Claudia and Jamie were not back, either.

I was right.

At long last I did what I'd been dreading. I called the community center. A very nice woman answered the phone. When I told her who I was and why I was calling, her tone became worried. "Mr. Braddock and several other parents have called during the last half hour," she told me. "We haven't seen the boats. And they should have been back by now. I think it's time to take some action."

"Um," I began, fear welling up inside of me, "do you think they got caught in that storm we had here awhile ago?"

"That's hard to say," the woman replied. "It depends on where it came from. If they *did* get caught in it, let's just hope they were already on Greenpoint."

"What kind of action are you going to take?" I asked.

"We'll call the Coast Guard and send out some search boats — I guess. It's going to be dark soon, and it's starting to rain again. Those aren't ideal searching conditions. Do you want to come to the center and help us?"

I did, but I had to say, "I'm really sorry, but I can't. My parents are away for the weekend. I have to stay here and take care of my baby brother."

"Okay," replied the woman. "Give me your phone number and we'll keep you posted."

"Thanks," I said. As I hung up the phone, it dawned on me: This was an emergency. My parents had left a long list of emergency numbers for the weekend. Most of them didn't apply — like the numbers for our pediatrician and the ambulance and the fire department. But I figured I should call Dr. Johanssen. The Johanssens are our neighbors and Becca is best friends with their daughter, Charlotte. Maybe they would watch Squirt for me so I could go to the center and help out.

I dialed the Johanssens' number. No answer.

I wanted to call the Pikes next — they'd be good in an emergency — but next on Mom's list of names and numbers was (gulp) my dreaded Aunt Cecelia. Aunt Cecelia is Daddy's older sister.

I can't stand her.

She wears smelly perfume and always looks as if she's just been eating a lemon. Her lips are permanently pursed. She disapproves of everything and treats Becca and me like absolute infants. Aunt Cecelia used to live in New Jersey with the rest of our relatives, but recently her husband died and she decided she couldn't live in their house anymore so she moved to *Queenstown, Connecticut*, which is much too nearby for my peace of mind.

If I called her and told her what was going on, I had a feeling she'd be over here as fast as if someone had *beamed* her to Stoneybrook.

I must have ESP. I was right about everything. In no time at all Aunt Cecelia zoomed up our driveway in her old Volkswagen, barged through the front door, and began saying (through pursed lips), "How could a couple of intelligent adults leave an eleven-year-old in charge of two younger children for three whole days? And how could you *and* your parents be irresponsible enough to let Rebecca go out on some sailboat?"

"It wasn't my fau — " I started to say, but Aunt Cecelia was already on the phone.

First she called the community center. "No news," she said curtly as she hung up. "I'll have to call your parents."

"My parents!" I exclaimed. "No! You'll ruin their vaca — "

"This is a serious matter, Jessica. It worries me that you don't understand that. Who knows what has happened to your sister? Your parents must be told what is going on."

Luckily, my parents were not in their hotel room, so Aunt Cecelia just left a message for them to call home. I had a reprieve.

As soon as my aunt hung up, the phone rang. I grabbed for it and got it before she did. (I think I took her by surprise.) I knew I was being rude, but I didn't care.

The caller was Mallory.

"Thank goodness it's you!" I exclaimed.

"Listen," said Mal, without asking why I sounded so relieved, "I want you to know that *we* know what happened. Mom and Dad and my brothers and even Vanessa are helping to search. Nothing's turned up yet. I thought you might like some company, though, so I arranged for Margo and Claire to go stay with Stacey's mom and I'm coming to your house. Right now. Okay?"

I was delighted, but I felt that it was only fair to warn Mal about Aunt Cecelia. Mallory said she didn't care, and proceeded to ride her bike over here in the rain. I was especially grateful for her company. Aunt Cecelia had taken complete charge of Squirt, dinner, and everything else. Without Mal, there would be nothing for me to do but worry.

Mal and I sat by the phone. At eight o'clock it rang. We jumped a mile. But it was only Kristy on the other end, saying that she was calling an emergency meeting of what was left of the BSC for the next morning — if no progress had been made in the search for the missing boaters.

CHAPTER 8

Dawn

Looking Back-
Saturday evening
Claudia and I knew we weren't on Greenpoint Island, but we weren't sure whether to tell the others. That was just a tiny dilemma, though. We had many more important matters on our minds as we stood, dripping and shivering, on the shore of the island. Like... what to do next. Find shelter? All I wanted to do was dry off, but I couldn't think how. Everything was wet. I was grateful to let Claudia take over.

The first problem that got solved was the smallest one, and it got solved by accident. Haley, who had been to Greenpoint several times with her family, looked around as the sky continued to brighten, and said, "You know something? We're on the wrong island!"

"What do you mean?" asked Jeff, glancing suspiciously at me.

"Well, um, she's right," I managed to say. "We blew off course."

"How much off course?" asked Jeff.

I looked at Claud. She shrugged. Then she said, "It doesn't matter. It won't help us to know. Come on, you guys. First order of business" (she sounded like Kristy) "is to find some sort of shelter. Then we'll build a fire and dry off and get nice and warm."

"Goody," said Haley, and then she began to sing, *"We're off to find a shelter!"* She sang it to the tune of "We're Off to See the Wizard" from the movie *The Wizard of Oz.*

"A wonderful shelter we'll find," added Haley.

Jeff and I loaded all the supplies from the boat into our arms, handing a few to Haley and Becca, and Claudia picked up the shivering Jamie.

We looked around. Where exactly were we

off to? The island had a nice beach. And the inland part looked dark and green, like a forest. I wondered how big the island was.

"Let's head for the trees," said Claudia.

Haley wanted to continue the song. *"We're off to find a shelter! A wonderful shelter we'll find. We hear there is a wonderful place, a wonderful, wonderful place. If ever a, ever a shelter there was, this island . . . um . . . this island . . ."*

That was as far as she got with her song. Becca didn't help her. She's too shy to sing in front of a bunch of people.

We headed into the trees but immediately backed out. The ground was drier in there, but the trees dripped on us and we didn't like the darkness at all. So we wandered along at the edge of the trees. All I could see behind me and ahead of me were beach and trees.

"Is this a *desert* island?" asked Haley, wide-eyed.

"I hope not," replied Claudia. "If it is, we're *way* off course. There are no desert islands off the coast of Connecticut."

"Deserted ones," I added, "but not actual desert islands."

"Gosh, well, anyway this is sort of like a book I read called *Baby Island*." Haley proceeded to tell us all about it.

That was when Jeff told us about *The Cay*.

And *that* was when Becca stopped in her tracks and said, "Hey, what's that? That hole over there?"

"That hole" turned out to be a cave. We'd come to a huge pile of boulders. That was the only way to describe them. They were the biggest rocks I'd ever seen. Great slabs of something (granite, maybe) all piled on top of each other. And three of them had formed a gigantic triangular space. It was high enough to walk into without bending over, and definitely wide enough and deep enough for six people.

Jeff and I set our supplies in the sand and turned on the flashlights.

"I guess we have to check this out, don't we?" I said nervously to Claudia. I was afraid of what we might find in the cave.

"Yeah," she said, looking at the sky, which was now growing dark again, and not just because evening was approaching. The sky was dark with clouds.

Cautiously, Jeff and I approached the cave. I glanced back once at Claudia, and she said, "Do you want me to go instead, Dawn?" I did — badly — but Jamie had laid his head on her shoulder and looked miserable, so I just said, "That's okay."

Jeff and I entered the cave. We shined our flashlights around as if we were expecting to find pirates guarding their treasure. Instead we found — nothing! Just the space between the boulders. And it was warm and dry.

"Hey, Claud! Come here!" I called to her.

Claudia, holding Jamie, ran to us, followed by Becca and Haley. They peered curiously inside, watching as Jeff and I aimed our flashlights into every nook and cranny.

"Do you think it's safe?" I asked Claudia.

She nodded. "These rocks have probably been here forever. I bet they're more solid than our houses back home."

So we unpacked our supplies, and then Jeff, Becca, and Haley looked around in the woods (but not too far away) for some dry sticks and leaves so we could start a fire. This was not easy, considering all the rain, and they were gone for quite awhile.

"I'm hungry," whined Jamie, so Claudia found him a still-dry peanut butter sandwich. (Thank goodness for Baggies.)

While he was eating it, Claud and I held a whispered, harried conversation at the other end of the cave.

"What are we going to do now?" I asked.

"Well, the boat's still in good condition," Claud replied.

"Yeah, but there's only one boat and there are six of us."

"I know. I was thinking that tomorrow, or whenever the weather clears, you and Jeff, or maybe Jeff and I, could take the boat, sail back to shore, and send the Coast Guard out here to rescue the others."

"Oh, Claud. I don't know. I mean, we don't know how far out we are, or if we can see the shore from here. And since we've walked partway around the island, we don't know which direction the shore is in. Whoever goes out in that boat could easily get lost at sea." I was nearly in tears. All I could really think about were the last words Mary Anne had spoken to me: "I wish I never had to see you again. I wish you would get out of my life — forever." Well . . . maybe I would.

Claudia put her arm around me. Then she whispered, "I know you're scared. I'm scared, too. But we don't want to frighten the kids." (She glanced over her shoulder at Jamie.) "So let's just pretend everything is okay. We'll talk about this later."

It began to rain again then, and just as I went to the cave entrance to call Jeff and the girls, they appeared, grinning broadly. Their arms were full of dry sticks, twigs, and leaves.

"We found them under this big rock that

stuck out," announced Haley proudly. "*Everything* under it was dry!"

The kids piled their findings in the center of the cave. Then we looked at each other. The same thought had occurred to all of us.

"How are we going to light it?" asked Becca.

"Rubbing two sticks together could take all night," added Jeff.

"I guess nobody has matches," I said unnecessarily.

For some reason, Jeff brightened at that.

"What? You've got *matches* on you?" I asked.

"Nope. But I bet there are some in the survival kit I found when you and I were taking all the stuff out of Claudia's boat."

We made a dash for our stash. Sure enough, there was a survival kit, containing exactly seven matches — and not much else. ("I'll have to speak to the people at the center about this," muttered Claudia.) But at least we got a fire going.

"Okay. Everyone dry out," I ordered.

We sat around the fire until we felt more comfortable.

"Now we better see about our food," said Claud. "Just in case we're here awhile, we've got to see how much of it can be saved, and then we better ration it — you know, eat a little at a time to make it last as long as pos-

sible." Jeff hauled the picnic baskets nearer to the fire, where we could see better. The baskets were soaked, of course, but he opened them up and found that we weren't in bad shape. The bottles of water, the big bottle of Coke, and the juice boxes were fine, of course. Warm, but fine. We set them in the coolest spot in the cave that we could find. The granola bars were soaked and had to be thrown out. The sandwiches in their Baggies were okay, but we decided to eat all of them for dinner, since we didn't know how long all-natural peanut butter and (ugh) bologna would last outside of a refrigerator. We decided to eat the salad for the same reason, and the yogurt, too, but we saved the bananas, apples, and candy bars.

"What if we ate all this food and had to start eating clams?" said Becca.

"Or grubs and worms?" said Haley, giggling.

"Snakes!" shrieked Jamie, and we laughed nervously.

Then Jeff said, "You know what? That Coke has been tossed around all day. Imagine what would happen if we opened it now!"

Nobody could stop laughing.

Then Jeff said, "I've changed my mind. This

isn't like *The Cay*. It's like *Gilligan's Island*. We're castaways!''

When we calmed down, we ate our dinner. I knew it was the last big meal we would have. We didn't even drink anything with it because I thought we should save our liquids as long as possible.

We sat around the fire. It was cozy — like camping out — and everyone seemed relaxed, except me. Mary Anne's words kept running through my head. I hoped she hadn't meant what she'd said. Whether she had or not, I promised myself that in the future I would try to be more responsible. Was this disaster a punishment for *not* being responsible? I wondered. Then I began to feel bad that *I* hadn't spoken to *Mary Anne* for so long. When (if?) I saw her again, I told myself that I would hug her, apologize, and never ''not speak to her'' again.

CHAPTER 9

Stacey

Notes for the BSC
Notebook - Saturday

It's like the old days. I'm back in New York City, and this afternoon I sat for my two favorite NYC charges, Henry and Grace Walker. Only now, since I'm a true member of the BSC again, I have to keep records of my sitting jobs and copy them into the club notebook when I get back to Stoneybrook.

It's a long weekend, so today there were plenty of special things to do, or to go to, with Henry and Grace. In fact, we had trouble deciding how to spend our afternoon, but at long last we chose a street fair not far from their apartment building (which used to be my old building, before Mom and Dad got divorced and both moved out).

Anyway, at the street fair was a ton of food stalls....

Stacey

Ring, ring! My note-keeping was interrupted by the telephone. I made a leap for it (my bedroom in Dad's new apartment is on the small side, so it wasn't much of a leap) and got to it before the third ring.

"Hello?" I said, hoping it was my New York best friend, Laine Cummings.

"Stacey? Hi, it's Kristy."

Kristy! She was about the last person I'd expected to hear on the other end of the line. In the first place, I wasn't expecting a long-distance call. In the second place, Kristy and I are good friends and all that, but we don't usually talk on the phone when I'm in New York.

"Hi," I said. "Is anything — "

"Stacey, I have bad news," Kristy interrupted me. "I thought you should hear about it right away."

A thousand thoughts ran through my mind. If Kristy was calling me, that meant that Claudia couldn't. Even though Kristy is the president of the BSC — and I assumed this had something to do with our friends and the club — Claudia would call me with bad news. Was Claudia sick or hurt?

"What happened?" I asked Kristy tightly,

and I realized that her voice sounded just as tight as mine.

"Claud and Dawn and the kids haven't come back from their race yet."

"Haven't come back," I repeated. "But it's almost seven o'clock! Shouldn't they have been home hours ago?"

"Well, awhile ago, that's for sure," said Kristy.

"Don't you think it's a good sign that *neither* boat has come back?" I asked. "I mean, if one boat sank, the other could still have returned. So wherever they are, they're together. I bet they're on the island."

"Maybe," replied Kristy doubtfully. "Someone will check that out soon. They could have crashed into each other, though. But the really scary thing is the weather we've been having. I don't know what it's like in New York — "

"Cloudy, but not bad," I told her.

"Oh. Well, here it started off nice, as you know, but we've been having showers and storms all afternoon. And we had one *huge* thunderstorm. If Claud and Dawn ran into that storm out on the water . . ."

Kristy didn't finish her sentence and she didn't need to.

"Oh, no," was all I managed to say.

"I know. It's awful. But the community center is starting a search, even though it's raining again, and the sky is almost as dark as nighttime. They're sending out boats and they've called the Coast Guard. Tomorrow, the Coast Guard will send out boats. They'll also send up helicopters and other small planes to search from the air. Mal's family is probably going to take some big boats out and look, and the people at the center say that if Claud and everyone haven't been found by tomorrow, then anyone who wants to can help by walking along the shore, looking for wreckage."

"Ew!" I said. "That's awful. I don't even want to think about wreckage."

"Listen," Kristy went on, "one reason I'm calling is to let you know that if they *haven't* been found by tomorrow, I'm calling an emergency BSC meeting for the morning. We'll hold it at Mallory's house. Do you think you'd like to come back for it? I know meetings are for discussing sitting problems, but to me, this — "

"They're also for club problems, aren't they?" I didn't wait for Kristy to answer. I just rushed on. "And this is a club problem. Two of our members are *missing*. I'll definitely try to be there. But I'll have to ask Dad first. And anyway, let's hope they're found and we won't need meetings or search planes or anything tomorrow."

"Right," said Kristy, still sounding grim.

Then a thought struck me. "How are Jessi and the Braddocks and the Kishis and everyone doing?"

"I guess as well as can be expected. Jessi'll probably have to call that aunt of hers, and her parents will probably come home. I haven't talked to her yet, though. It was Mrs. Kishi who called me with the news, and she sounded awful. She was *crying* over the phone." (Ooh, I hate it when adults cry.) "She's worried about Claud, of course, but I think she also feels responsible for Jamie and Becca, since they were in Claudia's boat. But mostly she just sounded as if she were in shock.

"Then," Kristy continued, "I called the Newtons to see if they needed me to come stay with Lucy if they wanted to be at the center. Lucy's too little to be hanging around there all night, and none of the BSC members are available except me. You're in New York, Claud and Dawn are, well, wherever, Jessi's stuck at home, Mal's keeping her company, and Mary Anne is keeping her father and stepmother company. That leaves me."

"How did the Newtons sound?" I asked. "Who did you talk to?"

"I couldn't reach them. I guess they're already at the center."

I sighed, thinking of all those distraught families — the Kishis; Dawn's new family, especially Mary Anne; the Braddocks; the Newtons; and the Ramseys.

"Oh, I wish Dawn and Mary Anne had been speaking to each other," I was saying, when a knock sounded at my door. "Hang on a second," I told Kristy. "Come in!" I called. Dad entered my room. He tapped his watch to remind me of the time. We had theater tickets for eight o'clock that night. "Kristy, I have to go, but I'll call you back in a little while, okay?"

"Okay."

I hated to hang up. It was like cutting off my last tie with Stoneybrook . . . and with Claudia.

"Honey," said Dad, sitting on my bed, "it's after seven and you're not dressed yet. We have to leave in less than half an hour."

"I can't go," I told my father flatly. "I have to get back to Stoneybrook tonight. It's really important." I told him what had happened.

"You can't leave tonight!" replied my father.

"You just got here this morning — and you're staying until Monday."

"But, Dad, these are my *friends*. I have to help find them."

"Stacey, I'm sure nothing horrible has happened to them. Even if there is a big search tomorrow, what can you do? You don't know anything about boats."

"I can ride around with the Pikes. Or I can join the search on the shore for the — wreckage."

"I really don't think you need to go," said Dad firmly. "Besides, we've got the theater tickets and it took me forever to get them. Furthermore, I never get to see you. Well, hardly ever. Well, not as often as I'd like. I miss you."

"And I'll miss Claudia and Dawn if anything has happened to them."

"That's a pretty big 'if,' Anastasia," said my father.

Whoa. *Anastasia*: It was time to back off. Dad only uses my full name when he's fed up with me.

"I'll get dressed," I said. I bet my lips were white. That's how mad I was. As soon as Dad left my room, I closed the door. I'm sure my father thought I just wanted the privacy, but I was *closing him out*.

Then, instead of changing, I called Kristy to tell her I couldn't come home. Then I called Laine Cummings and told her the whole story. Every word.

"Claudia and Dawn are *missing*," she whispered. "Wow. I don't believe it." (Laine knows my Stoneybrook friends.)

"Yeah. And Dad won't let me go back to Connecticut."

"That's pretty bad."

"He's just being selfish!" I cried. Then we had to get off the phone, since I really did need to change for the theater. But while I was getting dressed, all I could think about was my parents' stupid divorce. If they had behaved like grown-ups, worked out their problems, and stayed together, then I wouldn't be a divorced kid. I wouldn't be stuck with one parent in one place, while my friends were in trouble in another place. They needed me and I couldn't go to them.

I hate being a divorced kid.

Dawn

Looking Back—
Saturday Night

It was funny, but one thing that scared me a lot that first night on the island was looking down and discovering that my watch had stopped. It wasn't waterproof and it was ruined. Oh, no! I thought. We'll never know what time it is now! Isn't it weird—the kinds of things that freak you out? I mean, there I was, stranded on some island with a bunch of kids, and I was freaked out because I didn't know what time it was.

Claudia must have seen the look on my face because she reached over from where she was sitting and put her hand on my arm. "What's wrong?" she asked gently.

"Our watches!" I cried. "They've been ruined by the water. How will we be able to keep time?"

"Don't worry," said my brother. "*My* watch is waterproof." He checked it. "The time," he said grandly, "is exactly nine-oh-two."

I relaxed. I knew the time. And the kids and Claud and I were safe, warm, dry, and had full stomachs. Our fire was burning nicely, although we had to put sticks on it all the time to keep it going, and knew we would have to do that throughout the night. We were sitting around the fire in a circle, as if we were at camp. Jamie was in Claudia's lap, though, because we weren't sure he was old enough to know to stay away from the fire.

We'd been talking for quite awhile, the six of us, but it was odd; nobody mentioned our awful predicament. We talked about Kristy's softball team, about a test that Mary Anne and I would have to take at school the following week, and about what a pest Jamie thought Lucy was.

By the time we found out that it was nine

o'clock, though, we were beginning to fade. Jamie was almost asleep in Claudia's arms, and Becca's head was beginning to nod.

"I think," I said (and Becca came to), "that it is bedtime."

At home, probably any one of us would have given our parents a hard time about going to bed at nine o'clock, but the exhausted castaways agreed with me immediately. We had just one problem.

"What are we going to sleep on?" asked Jeff.

Sitting on the floor of the cave was one thing. Sleeping on it was another. It was dusty and cold, not to mention hard.

"Well," I said, "there's the blanket we packed for our picnic. That's still dry, thanks to Jeff."

Jeff grinned. He'd wrapped it in a tarp and tossed it onto Claud's boat.

In the cave, we had put the tarp-wrapped items next to the bottled water and Claud's candy bars. Now we unrolled each one until we came to the blanket. I spread it on the floor near the fire and Jeff lay down on it.

"Won't do," he said. "It's practically as hard as the cave floor. Just fuzzy. It's like lying on a really, really hard peach."

Becca and Haley giggled.

It took some thinking and experimenting,

but we finally hit on the idea of spreading out dry leaves (*not* too close to the fire) and lying on them with the blanket over us. This way we kept warm and were reasonably comfortable.

"Jeff," I said, "can you help Claudia and me keep the fire going tonight? We could use some help, and you've gone camping a lot."

"Sure," he replied. Ever since Jeff moved back to California, he has become one of the most easygoing, agreeable kids I know.

So we lay under the blanket, with our heads facing the fire, since Claudia said that her grandmother used to say, "Keep your head covered!" whenever it was cold out. And Becca added that Dr. Johanssen had told her that we lose the most body heat through our heads. We lay in this order: Me, Jeff, Becca, Haley, Jamie, Claudia.

Before we lay down, we moved our supply of kindling nearer the fire. "But how will we wake up to feed the fire?" I asked. I had a feeling that once the six of us lay down, we'd be out like lights.

"I'll set the alarm on my watch," answered Jeff.

"Are you sure it's working?" asked Claudia.

"No."

"Then maybe we should keep watches," she

said. "That might be a good idea in any case."

"What does that mean?" asked Jamie sleepily, and I knew he was confusing "keeping watches" with "wristwatches."

"It means . . . stay awake and make sure that, um, nothing happens. I mean, that we're safe."

"Safe from what?" asked Jamie, sounding more awake.

The six of us were snuggled into our nest, but the kids didn't seem so sleepy anymore.

"Safe from, oh . . ."

Claudia and I exchanged a Look, wondering how to get out of this mess.

"Bears?" asked Jamie, beginning to cry.

"Poisonous snakes?" asked Haley.

Next to me, even Jeff looked alarmed. "We don't know what's on this island," he said. "Maybe this cave belongs to a — "

I nudged him in the ribs before he could say anything too horrible.

"Maybe it belongs to a monster!" cried Becca.

"Oh, Becca. You don't really believe in monsters, do you?" asked Claud.

"Noooo," she said uncertainly. "But I'm afraid of the dark."

"Me, too," said Jamie, as Claud comforted him.

"Now come on, you guys." I tried to sound cheerful.

There was a silence. Then Haley said, "When will we be rescued?"

"I don't know," I answered honestly, "but I can tell you one thing. Everyone must be searching for us. We were supposed to be home this afternoon. Now it's almost ten o'clock."

"Are they looking for us in the dark?" asked Becca.

Again I had to say, "I don't know." But then I added, "They'll definitely be looking for us tomorrow."

"Then we can go home tomorrow!" exclaimed Haley.

"Well, only if they *find* us," Claudia pointed out. "We're not sure which island we're on."

"Oh. I see," was Haley's reply.

Another silence followed, and I allowed myself to think, Good. They're all going to sleep now.

I was fooled. The moment of silence was just the calm before the storm. Suddenly all four kids cried out at once:

"What if a rattlesnake slithers in here and bites us?" asked Haley.

"What if there really *are* monsters?" asked Becca. "Island monsters."

"I'm afraid of my dreams!" exclaimed Jamie.

And Jeff said, "What if we're in Nova Scotia or someplace? No one will *ever* find us! We're doomed."

Claudia and I started talking fast.

"We can't be *too* far from Stoneybrook," said Claud. "We didn't drift for very long."

"And if we're still near Connecticut, then we don't have to worry about rattlesnakes or other poisonous snakes. There aren't any around here," I pointed out.

"Plus, the fire will keep animals — and monsters — away," said Claudia.

"And if you think about nice things, then you'll have nice dreams," I told Jamie. "Now go to sleep, everyone."

After a few minutes, Claud whispered, "Dawn?"

"Yeah?"

"Come over for a sec so I can talk to you while the others are sleeping."

I wiggled out from under the blanket, walked around our bed, and sat on the cold floor next to Claudia. "What is it?" I asked.

"We should think about tomorrow," she said.

"Right," I agreed.

"We've only got two options as far as I can see. We could send a couple of us out in the boat, or we could wait here to be rescued."

"I guess. They don't sound like great choices, do they?"

"No," replied Claud uncertainly. "But we don't have to make a decision until tomorrow. We'll see what the weather is like. We'll walk around the island. Maybe we'll even be able to see land from somewhere. If we can, then going out in the boat will make more sense."

We talked a while longer. And then, dead tired, I tiptoed back to the other end of the bed. As soon as I got there, Jeff opened his eyes. "Even the people on *Gilligan's Island* were finally rescued," he whispered.

I grinned. "Go to sleep, Jeff," I said.

CHAPTER 11

Claudia

Looking Back—
Sundy Mourning

I didn't expet the iland to be brutiful but it was. It was very pretty. I realy felt like a caracter in a storybook. When we woke up, we looked all around. The wether had cleared up. The sky was blue agian. The only clouds were far away. And the kids were exited. They thot we would be found that day. Just one scary thing wehn we woke up. Jeff was gone.

"Where's Jeff?" were the first words I heard the next morning.

Dawn, Jeff, and I had spent the night keeping the fire going. Jeff had had the last watch. Now, as the rest of us woke up, we discovered that he was gone. Dawn was the one who had said, "Where's Jeff?"

I sat up in a hurry. I looked across our bed, which was a huge, leafy mess. There were Jamie, Haley, and Becca sitting up sleepily. And there was Dawn, standing up, looking panicky.

But Becca said, "I saw him tiptoe out of the cave a while ago."

"Are you sure?" asked Dawn.

"Positive."

"I bet he went exploring," said Becca.

"I hope so," replied Dawn. "I mean, I hope that's all he's doing."

Becca stretched, stood up, and walked to the entrance of the cave. "Whoa," she said. "It's a really nice day, even though it's hazy. But it's cold out there. Our cave is warm."

Dawn joined Becca at the cave entrance. "It is a nice day," she agreed. "I bet it will warm up later. Maybe the haze will burn off, too."

"You know what? It's almost *too* hot in here," said Jamie, looking flushed.

94

"It is pretty warm," I said. "But we better not let the fire go out. We'll be sorry tonight if we do. Besides, we don't have that many matches."

"I wonder what time it is," said Dawn. "My brother has skipped out with our only watch. I could ki — I mean, I wish he hadn't done that."

By that time we were all awake. And the more awake the kids got, the more excited they became. After last night, I'd expected them to greet the morning with fears, asking when we would be rescued, but Becca was excited about the weather, Haley was excited because she could see the water from the cave entrance, and Jamie dashed around crying, "We can go swimming later! It's nice enough to go swimming! And we all have our bathing suits with us. Isn't that *great*? Can I go swimming *now*?"

I shook my head. "No. But you can go later. After it's warmed up and after we've eaten our breakfast."

"What's for breakfast?" Haley wanted to know.

Dawn and I exchanged a glance.

"Well," said Dawn, "not a whole lot. You have a choice. Fruit or candy bars. I'm afraid that's it."

The kids looked a little bewildered.

Finally Jamie said, "No scrambled eggs?"

"I'm sorry," I told him. "Not unless you find a chicken on the island."

Jamie giggled.

Becca looked thoughtful. At last she said, "I love candy bars . . . but I've never had one for breakfast." She also looked a little naughty, as if she'd been told, "You can't have candy until after three o'clock in the afternoon," and now she was being given the opportunity of a lifetime. "I'll take the candy!" she cried suddenly. I'm sure she thought she'd never have the chance again.

"Me, too!" exclaimed Haley.

"*I* will have a banana," said Dawn.

"Me, too," said Jamie bravely.

"Well, I'm no fool," I said. "I'm going to have a candy bar."

"Or you guys could have fish," spoke up another voice.

We all turned toward the cave entrance. There stood Jeff, looking extremely proud of himself. He was grinning from ear to ear. And in his hands he held out some leaves on which he'd placed three small fish.

"How did you catch those?" asked Dawn, amazed.

"I'll show you later. It was easier than I'd

thought it would be." He held up a stick, attached to which was a length of string with an open safety pin tied to it. I guessed he'd found the things in the survival kit. "I would have caught more, but I figured you guys had woken up and were wondering where I was."

"We had and we were," said Dawn sternly, and I thought she was going to yell at him. Instead she said, "By the way, what time is it?"

"Nine o'clock," Jeff replied.

"It's always nine o'clock on this island," commented Dawn.

"I think we should name this island," said Jamie. "We'll call it Nine O'Clock Island."

"That's a stupid name," said Haley.

"Hey, come on, you guys," said Dawn. "With any luck, we'll leave the island today and we won't have to worry about naming it.

"Jeff, could you see land from your fishing spot?" asked Dawn.

"Nope," he replied. "Too hazy."

Dawn sighed. "Oh, well," she said. Then she went on, "Now look. Jeff's got three fish. We can cook them over the fire and have a nice, healthy breakfast."

"*Fish?*" squeaked Becca. "No way! I'm not eating fish."

"Me, neither," said Haley. "Not at break-fast. Not at any other time."

Dawn looked at Jamie, who had said he'd eat a banana. I guess the thought of a banana and fish for breakfast was just too much for him. He changed his mind entirely. "I'll have a candy bar!"

In the end, Dawn and Jeff divided the fish, cooking them over the fire, then eating one and a half each (they really were small), while the rest of us ate one candy bar each.

"This is good," I said, surveying our food supply as we sat around the fire with our breakfasts. "We still have most of the candy bars and the fruit — and Jeff can fish."

"*Now* can I have something to drink?" asked Haley.

"Just a little," replied Dawn. "I have this feeling that we should save our water and stuff. You can have half a juice box, okay?"

"Okay," replied Haley. She ended up split-ting the box with Becca.

Before we had finished eating, I said, "You know, Jeff, we're very grateful to you for the fish, but when Dawn realized you were gone, she was worried. We don't know our way around this island yet and I wouldn't want anybody getting lost. From now on, nobody should go anywhere alone — "

"Except *maybe* Claud or I," spoke up Dawn.

"Right," I said, "and nobody goes *any*where without telling Dawn or me first. Okay?"

"Okay," said Haley, Becca, Jamie, and Jeff.

"And no swimming without a buddy and a life preserver," added Dawn.

"A life preserver?" cried Jeff. "Just for *swim*ming?"

"Absolutely," replied Dawn. "Claudia and I are responsible for you guys and we aren't taking any chances."

Well, no one was very happy with Dawn and me for laying down rules, but they forgot their anger when Becca brightened suddenly and said, "I have got a *great* idea!"

"What?" cried the rest of us.

"Jeff, did you see any shells on the beach when you were fishing?"

"Tons," he replied. "Big ones. Clamshells, maybe. I think they washed up during the storm yesterday."

"Great," said Becca. "Listen, this is my idea: Since people think we're lost at sea, they'll probably be looking for us in boats *and* airplanes, right?"

"Right," we agreed.

"And we ought to let them know where we are, right?"

"Yeah?" we said tentatively.

"So what we do is gather up about a million of those clamshells and use them to spell out HELP as big as we can on the beach. Then people could see our message from the air."

"Becca, that's a terrific idea!" exclaimed Jeff. "Anyone would see that."

I wasn't so sure because of the haze, and I could tell that Dawn wasn't, either.

Becca's brilliant idea sounded like something she'd seen on TV. And she probably had. Seen it, I mean. On the other hand, Dawn and I hadn't come up with any better ideas. None that we wanted to try soon, anyway.

So we let the kids get carried away with enthusiasm. As soon as the day had warmed up, we stripped off our clothes (we were wearing our bathing suits underneath) and slathered on sunscreen. Then, keeping my promise to Mrs. Newton, I made Jamie put his windbreaker on. When we were ready, we followed Jeff to the beach near his fishing hole and there found the "tons" of clamshells.

"Oh, boy!" exclaimed Becca.

"Let's get to work," added Haley.

And so we began our first attempt at getting rescued.

CHAPTER 12

Kristy

Sunday Morning —
Emergency Meeting

Today was the first meeting of the BSC ever held at Mallory's house. (I took notes on it since this is a dire situation, and anyway, I am the president.) It was not a happy meeting. Two of our members are missing, and I mean actually missing, and a third member was absent. Stacey had called to say that her father wouldn't let her come home right away. She sounded really angry. We felt bad for her and wished she were with us, but we were more concerned with other things. Like -- exactly where are Dawn, Claudia, Jamie, Jeff, Becca, and Haley? ...

We have never held a meeting at the Pikes' house. In fact, I don't think we have held a Stoneybrook meeting anywhere but in Claudia's room. We held them there when we were all mad at each other and conducted meetings one person at a time so we wouldn't have to look at each other's faces. We held them there when Claudia was all caught up with this new friend of hers, Ashley Wyeth, and kept missing meetings. We even held them there right after Claudia's grandmother had died, because Claud had said she wanted her life to go on as normally as possible.

The point is, a meeting in Mal's room seemed very, very odd. She has no phone, but that didn't matter since we weren't lining up jobs. We were trying to decide what we could do to help find our vice-president, our alternate officer, and four kids we like a lot. The absence of Claud and Dawn was profound. (I read that word in a book and I like it a lot.) The absence of Stacey was noticeable, of course, but since we knew where she was, it didn't seem profound (at least not to me).

The four remaining members tried to make ourselves comfortable in the room that Mal shares with her sister Vanessa. Since there are two beds in the room, and only four of us were at the meeting, we all got to sit on beds for once. Mallory and I sat on one of the twin beds; Mary Anne and Jessi, looking absolutely awful, sat on the other. I don't think I've ever seen either one of them so shaken up.

Mallory and I were pretty upset ourselves. I even found it difficult to be official. So I didn't start the meeting by calling it to order. I just said, "Okay, you guys, this is an emergency meeting."

Before I could say anything more, Mary Anne, in her upset, said, "Oh, my gosh! Where's paper and a pencil? How am I supposed to take notes?" She was practically crying.

"Don't worry about it." I told her. "I'll take care of it." Mal handed me a notebook and a pen, and I started writing and talking at the same time, which is not easy to do.

"All right," I went on. "As I said, this is an emergency meeting. Claudia and Dawn are still missing."

At that point, Mary Anne really did begin to cry. She let loose a flood of tears, which set off Jessi. Mal and I were slightly surprised. Mary Anne cries at the drop of a hat, but Jessi hardly ever does.

Mal ran into the bathroom, returned with a box of Kleenex, and handed a huge bunch to

Mary Anne. She took some and passed the rest around.

"Anything could have happened to them!" wailed Mary Anne, and we all knew who she meant by "them." "Their boats could have capsized in that storm. They could have — "

"SHHH!" I nudged her in the ribs. "Jessi's *sister* is missing!" I hissed.

"Well, so's mine," replied Mary Anne, sniffling.

Oh, yeah. Sometimes I forget that Dawn and Mary Anne are stepsisters now, even though I have a stepsister of my own.

"And," Mary Anne continued in a wobbly voice, "I bet Jessi didn't tell *her* sister she never wanted to see her again. I did *not* mean that when I said it. Do you think this is some sort of punishment for being such an awful sister?"

"No," said Mal, Jessi, and I at the same time.

"You don't?" replied Mary Anne.

"Of course not," I said. "We all say things we don't mean."

"Like the time Nicky wished the triplets would turn into pigs," added Mal. "Do you think that actually *hap*pened?"

"No," said Mary Anne. "But this seems like more than coincidence."

"Well, did you say you wished you'd never

see Claudia, Haley, Becca, Jeff, or Jamie again?" I asked sensibly.

"No," Mary Anne answered. "Still . . . if yesterday really *was* the last time I saw my sister — I mean, um, alive — I'll feel terrible."

Jessi's sobs grew louder.

"Okay, you guys," I said sternly. (I felt bad being stern in these circumstances, but somebody had to do it.) "I know the situation doesn't look great, but would everyone be out searching if they really thought that Dawn and Claud were — I mean, if they really thought there was no point?"

"No," said Jessi and Mary Anne feebly.

"Absolutely not," said Mal, and I gave her a thank-you smile.

"Well, that's why we're here today," I went on. "What can we do to help search? Or at least to help the Newtons and the Braddocks and the Kishis and everyone through this tough time?"

"How *are* the Newtons and the Braddocks and the Kishis doing?" asked Mal.

"About as well as my dad and stepmother and Jessi's family are," replied Mary Anne. "And about as well as Mr. Schafer would be doing if he knew what was going on, but he doesn't. We can't reach him. I think he's away for the long weekend."

Jessi groaned. "You know what?" she said. "Sorry this is off the subject, Kristy, but I have to tell you guys. Mom and Dad are on their way home."

"Oh," moaned Mal. "Their vacation is ruined."

"Yeah. And Aunt Cecelia has completely taken over our house. She's caring for Squirt, and for some reason, she's cleaning like a demon. You'd think she'd be out searching."

"The Braddocks, the Newtons, and the Kishis are searching," spoke up Mary Anne. "My mom spoke to Mrs. Newton, Mr. Braddock, and both of Claud's parents last night. Someone's watching Lucy Newton all day today, and Mr. and Mrs. Newton are out on a Coast Guard boat. The Braddocks, even Matt, are combing the shore for any sign of debris. So are the Kishis. And my dad and Sharon are helping coordinate things at the center. I think the searching and helping is, like, therapy. It keeps everyone from going crazy."

"So what can we do?" I asked for the fifty millionth time.

"*I* want to go out on a boat and search, but there's no way Aunt Cecelia will let me do that," said Jessi. "I'm in major hot water with her. She thinks I'm the one to blame, even though Mama and Daddy gave Becca permission to go sailing. She is so unfair. You know what? I hate my aunt."

"So you're stuck here," I said. "Do you think your aunt would let you check the shoreline?"

Jessi sighed. "I don't know. I don't want to be at home with that — that *bat*." (I almost giggled.) "On the other hand, she almost didn't let me come here, so she probably won't let me help search."

"What about you, Mal?" I asked.

"Oh, I'll be out on a big motorboat with my parents and probably the triplets by this afternoon. We've canceled our plans so we can go searching. It won't be easy trying to see through this darn haze, but any of you can join us. It seems like practically all of Stoneybrook is looking for Claud and Dawn and Becca and everyone."

For some reason, tears came to my eyes then. I'm not a crier. In fact, I'm the opposite of Mary Anne. But every now and then something moves me. Suddenly I was thinking of all the sad families — the distraught parents, the bewildered brothers and sisters — and I couldn't keep my tears to myself. Mallory handed *me* a bunch of Kleenex, and then needed to use some herself. I guess the sight of the rest of us crying was too much for her.

She hugged Jessi, and I hugged Mary Anne.

After several minutes, Mary Anne blew her nose and said, "I just don't think I can help with the search. It might be therapy, but I wouldn't be able to keep my mind on it. I know it's childish, but all I can think of are the horrible things I said to Dawn."

"And Stacey won't be able to help," I added as my tears dried. "Not unless her father springs her from New York."

"What about you, Kristy?" asked Mallory. "Do you want to come out in the boat with my family? We'd be glad to have you."

I started to say, "Sure!" when I remembered something. "Uh-oh," I said instead. I felt my face flush.

"What?" asked the others.

"I just remembered. I scheduled a Krushers' practice for this afternoon."

"So cancel it," said Mal.

"I can't. I mean, it's not that easy. We've got a game tomorrow. We purposely scheduled one for the Monday holiday, and the Krushers have really been looking forward to it. They think they might *finally* beat the Bashers. I think so, too. I'd hate to let them down. I've got responsibilities to them."

"You've got responsibilities to your friends, too," said Jessi softly.

"You're right," I replied. Then I paused. "I don't know what to do. It's not fair to let the kids down. The boating disaster doesn't have anything to do with them, except that Haley and Jamie won't be at the game."

"Are you sure it's not Bart you're afraid of letting down?" asked Mary Anne. She always manages to get to the heart of the matter where matters of the heart are concerned. See, I go out with Bart Taylor sometimes. He just happens to be the coach of the Bashers.

I thought for a moment. At last I said, "You know what? You're right, Mary Anne. I don't want Bart to think I'm chickening out. And that's about the worst reason I can come up with for not going with Mal today. I'll call Bart and cancel tomorrow's game. Then I'll have Sam or someone help me cancel the Krushers' practice for today."

"Let's give Stacey one more call to see if she can come home early," suggested Mary Anne.

So we did, but she couldn't.

After that I called Sam to give me a hand with canceling practice.

And *then* I picked up the phone (in privacy) to call Bart.

CHAPTER 13

Dawn

Looking Back —
Late Sunday Morning

You know what was wrong with spelling HELP with shells? The shells were about the same color as the sand. Claudia and I realized early on in the project that no one would be able to see our message, especially from as far away as up in a plane. The only thing a searcher would see was a stretch of white at the edge of an island. Even from down the beach, Claud and I couldn't tell the clam shells from the sand. But we didn't let the kids know that. We simply realized that if we were going to be rescued, we'd have to work harder, or do something more drastic....

Well, if nothing else, spelling out our message put the kids in good spirits. So did the planes we could hear, but not see through the fog and haze. The kids were sure we'd be rescued later that day.

"We're working really hard!" Jamie yelled to Claud and me at one point.

"That's terrific!" I shouted back.

The reason we were shouting was that Claud and I were finishing up the H and Jamie was finishing up the P, and our all-white disaster signal was so big we were pretty far apart.

"And guess what!" Jamie went on.

"What?" yelled Claud.

"Now I know how to spell *six* words: Jamie, Lucy, Mommy, Daddy, love, and *help!*"

Jamie roared the last word, and the rest of us laughed. Despite what Claudia and I had realized about our message, even the two of us were in better spirits. It was weird, but in spite of our *awful* predicament we weren't feeling too bad at that point. Wandering along an island beach in our bathing suits was pleasant. We were almost able to forget that we were shipwrecked castaways.

When HELP was finally finished (and it took a long time to create) the kids wanted to do the things they'd missed out on the afternoon before — namely swim, explore (cautiously), play games, and, now, learn to fish.

"I just want you to know," Haley made a point of telling Claudia and me as she was about to go to Jeff's fishing spot, "that I *still* won't eat fish. Not now, not ever."

"That's okay," Claud told her. "I'm no fan of fish myself. Especially when I see them alive before I eat them."

I rolled my eyes.

Claudia and I played lifeguard for about an hour while Becca swam in the ocean and patiently tried to teach Jamie the sidestroke. Jamie worked hard but it's difficult to learn the sidestroke while wearing a life preserver. He kept rolling over. At least he and Becca thought that was funny. Becca finally began pretending that Jamie was her pet puppy. She'd shriek, "Roll over!" and Jamie would because he couldn't help it.

Claudia and I laughed until our stomachs ached.

"I wonder what time it is," I said as we got our breaths back.

Claud looked at me like I was crazy. "What is it with you and time?" she asked. Then she quickly added, "I bet it isn't nine o'clock."

I smiled. "I'm just wondering how long the

kids have been in the water. It isn't all that warm."

"Oh, you're right," said Claud. "Hey, Becca! Jamie! Come on back here!"

Reluctantly, our two swimmers waded ashore. Jamie's lips were blue and his teeth were chattering.

"Uh-oh," said Claud. "I promised Mrs. Newton I'd keep Jamie warm. Here, Jamie. Put on your windbreaker."

"Yuck," said Jamie. But he put it on anyway.

At that point, Haley and Jeff returned, looking pretty proud of themselves.

"Lunch!" Jeff called, dramatically holding out several more small fish for Claud and me to see.

"Yum," I said.

"Ew," Claud said.

"Wimp," I teased her.

"Dawn? Can we build a fort?" asked Jeff, after checking his watch for me. "You know, we might need one. The cave is good shelter, but it's sort of damp and cold. And we don't know how long we're going to be — "

Jeff stopped when I gave him the evil eyeball.

"You mean building a fort might be lots of fun?" spoke up Claud.

"Oh. Yeah," said Jeff.

"Of course you can," I told the kids. All four of them were crowded around, waiting for an answer.

"Yea!" they cried.

"But stay right at the edge of the woods where we can see you," said Claud.

The kids ran off, and Claudia and I sat down against a boulder. We watched Jeff instruct the others on fort-building.

"He's really good with kids," remarked Claud after awhile.

"I know," I said. "I discovered that the last time I was visiting in California. Jeff and I got stuck sitting for two kids one night, and the baby wouldn't stop crying. So I took care of the baby and Jeff entertained the older kid. He was great."

"It's good to know," said Claud slowly. "I mean, if anything happens to you or to me, I think Jeff could kind of take over."

I didn't answer. The thought was too frightening.

We watched as the fort-building continued. The kids were having a lot of fun, but they weren't making much progress.

"You know," Claudia said as Haley and Becca tried to lash some sticks together with damp vines, "we're just putting it off."

"Putting what off?" I asked.

"Finding the boat."

I sighed. "Yeah."

"Because when we find it," Claud went on, "then we'll have to decide what to do. Like whether to send a couple of people off in it."

I sighed again. Then I said, "Let's go right now."

"Now?"

"Why not? The kids aren't near the water and I trust Jeff to be in charge. If I tell him to keep the others out of the water and not to go any further into the woods than they are right now, he'll do what I say."

"Okay." Claud got to her feet and dusted the sand off of her bathing suit.

"Jeff?" I shouted.

"Yeah?"

"Come here for a sec."

Jeff ran across the beach to Claud and me. He listened seriously as I told him what we were going to do. Then he promised to keep the others entertained and to follow my instructions.

So Claudia and I set off down the beach. We walked and walked.

"I don't remember coming this far yesterday," I said after awhile.

"Neither do I," said Claudia. "You know

what? I think we've come too far. I don't remember that gnarled tree." She pointed toward the woods.

"Maybe we went in the wrong direction," I suggested.

"No. I'm sure we went the right way."

Claudia and I had walked about halfway back to the kids when the same thought struck us at the same time.

"Oh, my lord," whispered Claudia.

"The boat washed away, didn't it?" I said.

"I guess so. I bet we landed at low tide." Claudia smacked her hand to her forehead. "How could we have been so stupid?"

"We didn't know," I pointed out. "We didn't know it was low tide."

"Yeah, but we should at least have pulled the boat inland a little."

"Well, we didn't."

"Now what?" asked Claud. "That boat was the only way for us to leave the island."

"Not a very good way, though. Not safe. And we can't see land because of this darn haze. Why won't the weather clear up? No one will be able to see us, will they?"

"No," admitted Claudia.

"So we couldn't have sailed off. We wouldn't have known where we were going. We would probably have ended up adrift."

Claudia sank down in the sand then.

"What? What is it?" I asked, sitting beside her.

"I just thought of something. Your boat got wrecked yesterday. I think we can be sure of that. And my boat just floated away. I'm sure people are out searching today, but when they find one wrecked boat and one empty boat, what will they think?"

"The worst," I replied.

Claudia nodded. "Oh, I hope they don't stop searching."

"I bet they won't. Not right away," I said.

But Claudia didn't believe me. Even *I* didn't believe me. And although I'm usually known for being calm and unflappable, I burst into tears right there on the beach. I cried and cried. Claudia tried to comfort me, but at that moment, it was impossible. All my guilt over Mary Anne came flowing out, along with about a hundred other worries including, of course, our predicament.

"Dawn," said Claudia finally, "we have to go back to the kids."

"I know."

"And they'll get upset if they see that you're upset."

"I know."

120

"Can you stop crying?"

"Yes," I replied, and I did.

We walked along the beach and found Jeff leading Haley, Becca, and Jamie in a game of tag. He ran to us as soon as he saw us.

"What did you find?" he asked.

I told him.

"Too bad," he said, frowning. Then he pointed to the sky. "I don't want to scare anyone, but . . ."

I looked up. Another storm was brewing.

CHAPTER 14

Mary Anne

Sunday Afternoon
I had forgotten that I
had a sitting job with
Charlotte Johanssen this
afternoon. Completely forgotten. And I'd lined it
up myself, since I'm the
club secretary. Luckily
Dr. Johanssen phoned me
about an hour before the
job, wondering if I still
wanted to baby-sit. She
knew that Claud and Dawn
and everyone were missing
(the whole town knew it)
and that I might want to
search instead of sit. But I
decided to go for the baby-

sitting. I hoped it would take my mind off of both the disaster and my problems with Logan....

As you can imagine, Dad and my stepmother were nearly hysterical about Dawn and Jeff. Sharon wasn't just worried that her kids were missing. She also kept saying things like, "Oh, they're going to take custody away from me and I'll never see Dawn again. Jeff will never even be allowed to visit here." And Dad kept saying things like, "It's not your fault."

At least Sharon thought that everyone would be found. Even so, she continued to make frantic calls to Mr. Schafer in California. He wasn't home, though. And if he had an answering machine, it wasn't on. We had no idea where he was.

When I got home from our emergency BSC meeting, Dad and Sharon were gone. They were at the community center.

What was I going to do with myself for the rest of the day, I wondered? I was beginning to feel guilty about not searching. Just then, the phone rang.

News! I thought. (That was what I'd thought every time the phone had rung since last night.)

I raced for the phone. "Hello?" I said breathlessly.

"Mary Anne?"

Logan?! Nah, it couldn't be.

"This is Logan," said Logan.

I was speechless. Logan and I hadn't talked to each other since our fight. I'd been too chicken to call him, and I was certain he was too angry to call me.

"Are you there?" asked Logan.

"Oh. Oh, yeah," I said brightly.

"Look, I just wanted to say that I'm really sorry about the boating, um, the boating . . ."

It was funny, but nobody really knew what to call the tragedy, since we didn't know what had happened. The boating disappearance? The Case of the Missing Boaters?

"Thanks," I replied. Was Logan making up with me? Or was he just being polite and concerned? After all, he's a member of the BSC, and he knows Claud and Dawn pretty well. He sees them at school every day.

"Any news?" he asked.

"No." My voice wobbled.

"Are you going to help search?"

"I don't think so. You know I'm no good in . . . I don't know." I didn't feel like telling Logan that Dawn and I hadn't been speaking to each other, either. Then I made up a huge lie. "I thought," I said, "that I'd stick around in case anyone needed me. The Braddocks and the other families are torn to pieces over this." (Well, that much was the truth.) "Someone might need a sitter. . . . Logan?"

"Yeah?"

"Does this mean our fight is over?"

"Does what mean our fight is over?"

"This phone call," I said. "You're speaking to me."

There was a long pause. "No. It doesn't."

I felt a rock forming in my stomach. I *hate* having people mad at me. "Why not?" I knew I sounded pathetic.

"Because I *still* can't believe that you thought I'd stood you up. I would never do that. And if you don't know that, then you don't know *me* very well."

Uh-oh. What had I walked into? "I'm sorry," I said.

"Me, too," answered Logan.

And then he hung up.

I had already cried so much about Dawn and Claudia that I didn't have any tears left in me. And under ordinary circumstances, Logan's hanging up on me would have been a terrific opportunity for a good cry. But I couldn't do it.

I stared into space for awhile.

I found Tigger, pulled him into my lap, and patted him for awhile.

I tried calling Mr. Schafer again, but couldn't reach him (again).

I considered cleaning the house, but decided I wasn't quite that desperate. So I went back to staring into space.

That had been going on for fifteen minutes or so when Dr. Johanssen called me. "Are you *sure* you want to baby-sit this afternoon?" she asked.

"Positive," I replied. "I need something to do." Something other than staring.

"I'll warn you. This isn't going to be an easy job. Charlotte is very upset about Becca. We tried to convince her to come on Mr. Johanssen's company picnic with us, but she looked at us as if we were crazy."

"Well, she and Becca *are* pretty close," I said. "Anyway, don't worry. Charlotte and I will be fine."

"All right," said Dr. Johanssen uncertainly.

An hour later I was ringing the Johanssens' bell.

Charlotte answered the door, looking as listless as an old rag.

"Hiya," I said.

"Any news?" was Charlotte's reply.

I shook my head. "I'm sorry." Dad and Sharon hadn't even called by the time I'd left the house. (I'd placed a gigantic note in the kitchen where they couldn't miss it. The note said I was sitting for Charlotte. I didn't want them to think that I was missing, too.)

"Come on inside," said Mr. Johanssen from behind Charlotte.

And for some reason, those words caused Charlotte to burst into tears.

"Oh, sweetie," said her father. He gave her a hug as I edged into the house. "I bet they'll find Becca today. I bet they'll find everyone."

"She's my best friend," wailed Charlotte.

"I know she is. And I know you're worried. Everyone is searching."

"That's right," I told Charlotte. "And not just the Coast Guard. The Kishis and the Braddocks and the Newtons and my friends. They're all looking. The Pikes and Kristy even went out on a big boat."

Charlotte's tears subsided.

"Are you sure you don't want to come on the picnic with us?" asked Mr. Johanssen. "It would take your mind off of — "

"No," interrupted Charlotte, "and I don't know how you can go, either."

Whoa. If I'd said that to Dad . . . major trouble. But the Johanssens just said good-bye to us and left. Charlotte and I were still stand-ing by the front door. She looked at me with huge eyes.

"Hey, Char," I said, inspired, "would you feel better if you could see the search that's going on?"

Charlotte shrugged. "I've seen it on TV."

I'd seen the broadcasts, too. We were mak-ing news. The local networks were covering *only* the search, and little old Stoneybrook even made spots on national news. The local channels called the tragedy the *Connecticut Dis-aster*. They placed round-the-clock newscasters at the center, on the beach, and even on the Coast Guard boats. They interviewed every-one and kept asking them how they felt. One of them had made the mistake of asking Sharon how she felt, now that two of her chil-dren were missing. Guess what she replied. She snapped, "How do you *think* I feel?"

I had not seen her on the *Connecticut Disaster* coverage yet.

"Look," I said to Charlotte, "I've seen the search on TV, too, but somehow I have a feel-ing that's not the same thing. Let's look at it up close. Do you feel like riding your bike to the community center?"

"It's a long ride," said Charlotte slowly, but

I could tell she was warming up to the idea.

"Come on. Get your bike. I rode mine over here."

"Well . . . okay!" Charlotte looked like she wanted to be excited about our adventure, but didn't think she ought to be. Was she afraid of having fun while her best friend was missing? Probably.

We rode to the community center, taking the fastest route I knew. On the way, we passed a WATL van.

"Ooh," said Charlotte. "There are the newspeople."

When we neared the center, we saw that it was so crowded with searchers and families and "newspeople" that we had to chain our bikes to a lamppost two blocks away and walk to all the excitement.

"Wow! Look up there!" exclaimed Charlotte just as we reached the center.

I looked up — and saw two small planes taking off.

"See?" I said. "They really are doing everything they can to find Becca and the others."

Charlotte nodded, awed.

"There's my dad," I said to Charlotte as we opened the doors.

Dad looked up as we entered the crowded

room, but he couldn't talk to me. He was busy
on the phone. He waved to me, though. I
think he was glad I'd come.

"Let's go out to the docks," I suggested.

And just then a microphone was thrust in
front of Charlotte and me. "Are you friends
of the missing?" asked a deep voice. It belonged to a WATL newscaster.

Charlotte and I looked at each other. "Yes,"
I answered in a small voice.

"And how do you feel right now?" he went
on.

I drew myself up. "How do you *think* we
feel?" I replied.

The man backed off and Charlotte had to
bite her lips to keep from laughing.

As soon as we were outside on the docks I
said to Charlotte, "I just blew our shot at being
on television. I hope you don't mind."

Charlotte shook her head. "You were
great!" she cried.

I was glad to have done one great thing that
day.

Charlotte and I stayed on the dock until
about a half an hour before her parents were
due back. We saw planes flying low overhead.
We saw Coast Guard boats and volunteer
search boats. We even saw the Pikes and
Kristy. They docked late in the afternoon.

Everyone got off the boat looking discouraged. Mallory was crying.

"We didn't see anything. Not a thing," she said. Her mother gave her a quick hug.

"Well," I said quickly, "I think that's a good sign. Don't you, Kristy? At least you didn't find any wreckage."

"Yeah," agreed Kristy. "No news is good news."

"Right." I squeezed Charlotte's hand. "Come on. We better get going."

Charlotte and I rode home silently, each thinking our own thoughts. I know we were impressed by the search efforts. But we were disappointed and worried by the lack of news.

CHAPTER 15

Dawn

Looking Back—
Sunday Afternoon and Night
As long as I live, I hope I
never have to go through another
night like Sunday night. I know
this sounds dramatic, but I
truly think it was the most
desperate one I've ever spent.
Not only hadn't we been rescued,
but our food was just about gone
and we had a sick child on our
hands. Exactly what we needed.
Claudia and I dragged up
everything we knew about first
aid, but there wasn't much we
could do without medicine, a
thermometer, or ice. What we
really needed was a phone so we
could call a doctor.

By the end of Sunday, everyone was flagging. The kids had been in high spirits earlier, but now their spirits had dropped right down into the dumps. They were tired of fishing and exploring and swimming and building huts. They were even tired of candy bars, which I took as a very bad sign.

At about five o'clock (Jeff Schafer time) we headed back to the cave. We'd been running to and from it all day — getting food, escaping from rain, keeping the fire going — but I knew that this would be our final trip there for the day. The kids and Claudia looked exhausted. I'm sure I did, too.

"I think we're going to have a nice sunset," said Jeff, trying to sound cheerful.

I looked at the sky. It had been cloudy, then just hazy, then cloudy, then hazy all afternoon. And we'd had one tremendous thunderstorm about twenty minutes after Jeff had pointed out the dark clouds that morning. But now the sky was clear. And the sun was sinking. We probably would have a nice sunset.

"You know what?" said Haley, who was lagging behind us.

"What?" I asked, turning around.

"I think it's weird that we haven't been rescued yet. Why hasn't anyone found us?"

"Because they just haven't," answered Claudia before I could say anything.

"Then something is wrong. How far from Greenpoint do you think we are?"

"I honestly don't know," said Claud.

"Hey, where's our boat?" asked Jamie crossly. He had said he was too tired to walk, so Jeff was giving him a piggyback ride.

Claudia and I exchanged a nervous glance.

"It's sort of gone," I replied.

"What do you mean?" asked Becca, narrowing her eyes at me. "How could it be *sort of* gone?"

"Okay, it's completely gone," I told the kids. "It washed away during the night. We should have dragged it further up the — "

And right then and there, quiet, sensible, mature Haley threw a temper tantrum. She'd been standing near the cave entrance when suddenly she dropped to her knees and began pounding the sand with her fists. "Get the boat back! Get the boat back!" she screeched.

"Haley — " began Claudia.

Jamie finished her sentence for her. "Go to your room," he commanded, but his voice sounded weak. And he looked only mildly interested in Haley.

The rest of us trooped into the cave, leaving Haley and her temper outside to cool off.

Becca was still giving Claudia and me cross looks, so I said to her, "We couldn't have used the boat anyway. Six of us can't fit in it, and besides, we wouldn't know what direction to take if we sailed away. We'd just have gotten lost. At least we've got shelter on the island. . . . Did you hear that, Haley?" I shouted.

"Yes," she replied, stepping guiltily into the cave.

"Boy, is he warm," said Jeff, letting Jamie slip off his back and to the ground. "He's like a hot water bottle."

Claudia and I turned away from Haley and Becca and looked at Jamie. His face was flushed, his eyes were bright, and he seemed awfully tired.

In an instant, Claud and I had both put our hands on Jamie's forehead.

"He's got a fever," said Claud.

"A high one," I added. "How high do you think it is?"

"A hundred and three?" guessed Claudia.

I nodded.

"Oh, brother," said Jeff.

"Jamie? Do you feel okay?" I asked him carefully. I didn't want to put any ideas in his head.

"Not really," he replied.

"What's wrong?" asked Claud.

135

"I hurt. I hurt all over. Especially my head. And my throat is sore. And my ear aches."

Claud and I glanced at each other over the top of Jamie's head.

"What do you think he has?" I wondered.

"The flu?" suggested Claudia.

"Maybe. Do you get an earache with the flu? I hope it isn't an ear infection."

Claudia sighed. "Okay, she said. "Jamie, you're going to have a special bed tonight. Over here, away from the others. Dawn and I will stay with you."

"Thank you," said Jamie politely, and as soon as a "bed" had been prepared for him, he sank onto it and fell asleep.

"What's for dinner?" asked Becca a little while later.

"Fish!" said Jeff.

"Candy bars," said Claudia.

The kids looked sort of green at both possibilities.

"Hey," said Claud, "come on. There are three candy bars left. We can divide them up. . . . Mmm. Mounds bars. Yummy."

But the thought of *more* candy was too much for the kids. And the thought of fish still grossed them out, even after Jeff had cooked some up for himself and for me.

"It's their *eyes*," said Becca. "How can you

stand to look them in the eye, then fry them up and *eat* them?''

''Because we'd rather do that than be hungry,'' replied Jeff.

But Becca, Haley, and Claudia chose hunger over fish that night. And Jamie, whose stomach was empty, too, just drifted in and out of sleep while the others talked, scared themselves with ghost stories, and played word games.

Claudia and I sat worriedly on either side of the sleeping Jamie.

''What should we do?'' asked Claud at one point, her hand on his cheek. ''He feels warmer than ever. Boy, what I wouldn't give for some children's Tylenol right now. Or better yet, a doctor.''

''Maybe he's got a virus,'' I said. ''You know, you're supposed to be able to flush a virus out of someone with water.''

Claudia looked skeptical. ''I don't know about that,'' she said, ''but if he's got a fever, then he *should* have liquids. That's one thing we can do for him.''

''You're right!'' I cried. ''And we've still got all the bottled water. I had a feeling we should be saving that.'' I jumped up, got the water and also the remaining juice boxes, and brought them to Jamie's nest. ''I think we should wake him up and make him take a drink. We should probably do that all night."

"We'll use up all the water that way," said Claud.

I paused. "I know," I said finally, "but it's the only thing we can do for him."

So we woke up poor Jamie and made him drink about half a cup of water.

"It's good for you," I told him.

Jamie coughed and went back to sleep. About an hour later he woke up. "Dawn?" he said, "I'm freezing," and he began to shiver violently.

"Great," said Claud. "Now he's got a fever *and* chills. . . . Hey, you guys," she called to the others, who were getting ready to go to sleep. "I hate to say this, but we need your blanket over here."

It's to their credit that the other kids immediately surrendered the blanket. Then they inched closer to the fire and burrowed under the leaves. It was the best they could do. Not one of them complained. And Jeff even said, "Call me if you need me," before he drifted off to sleep.

The longest night of my life had begun.

I sat with Jamie while Claud napped a little. Then I woke Jamie up to give him some more water.

"Oh!" he cried. "Stay away!" I had a feeling he didn't mean me. Sure enough, the next words out of his mouth were, "It's a tiger! It's a tiger!"

I gave him the water anyway. When he had finished drinking, he kicked off the blanket. "I'm so *hot*," he murmured, but soon he was shivering again. We needed *half* a layer of blanket.

"Stop! Snake!" Jamie cried out.

"Claud, wake up," I whispered.

"Mmm." She rolled over sleepily.

"I think Jamie's delirious."

That woke her up. "What?" she said, sitting up. "Delirious?"

"He's crying out in his sleep. Stuff about tigers and snakes."

"Maybe he's just dreaming."

"I hope so," I said. "How can you tell the difference?"

"I don't know."

"Claud? What if we catch this from Jamie? What are the others going to do if we both get sick?"

Claudia thought for a moment. She rubbed her eyes. "Do you think Jeff can manage the little kids all by himself? He *is* pretty responsible."

"Yeah, I think he could manage them. Uh-oh. What if the *kids* get sick? All of them? Can we nurse four kids? Or what if — "

"Dawn, stop thinking about the 'what-ifs.' You're making me crazy. Really. And you're overlooking something important."

"What?"

"We might get rescued. We could all be home by tomorrow night."

Home. Where there were doctors and mothers.

"You know what I want more than anything right now?" I whispered.

Claudia shook her head.

"My mom," I said.

"Me, too."

But we couldn't have our moms, so I took a nap. I woke up when Jamie began shrieking about snoring trees. I gave him some water. Then Claudia napped. All night, we took turns napping, keeping the fire going, and caring for Jamie. I didn't think our patient was getting any better, though.

CHAPTER 16

Claudia

Looking Back —
Monday Morning

The frist thing I did wehn I woke up on monday was fell Jamie's forhead. It was much cooler I felt releeved. I hopped the worst was over becuase we had no more water left for anyboddy. There was nothing to drink! Even our soda was gone. I almost paniced. Then I thoght, well mabe we can colect rain water somehow. But do you know why that was a scary thoght? Becuase it meant we had to survive now realy survive. And that meant hard work and using our breians Also we could use some luck.

At six o'clock on Monday morning (I knew it was six because Dawn tiptoed over to her brother and looked at his watch), Dawn said, "I'm beat. Can you stay up for awhile, Claud?"

I was just waking from a nap. "Sure," I replied groggily.

"Good," said Dawn. She immediately rolled over and fell asleep.

That was when I felt Jamie's forehead.

"Oh, good," I said aloud. "Much cooler."

Jamie was sleeping peacefully. He hadn't cried out in several hours. Maybe the worst was over. And maybe, just maybe, you really could flush a virus out of someone. After all, he'd drunk two whole bottles of water and had been to the bathroom about six times.

I tiptoed to the cave entrance. The sky was still gray, but I could see that it was gray with looming clouds as well as with dawn. Great, I thought. Another storm was coming. We needed another storm like we needed extra feet.

"Claudia?" whispered Becca from her nest.

"Yeah?" I knelt beside her.

"Is Jamie okay?"

"He's much better. Don't worry about him. Are you okay?" I had taken one of Becca's hands, and it was freezing.

"Just a little cold," said Becca. "I think I'll go back to sleep."

"Sorry about the blanket," I told her.

"That's okay. Jamie needs it."

Becca nestled under the leaves and fell asleep.

For the next hour, I puttered around the cave. We had been careful to keep our trash in one place so we wouldn't litter the island. I actually neatened our trash! I bet even Mary Anne's tidy, precise father has never neatened trash. Then I stoked the fire again, thought about escaping from the island, and checked Jamie. He was still cooler than last night. I didn't think his temperature was normal, but it wasn't anything to be too concerned about.

About an hour later, everyone began to get up.

The first words out of Jeff's mouth were, "I don't believe it. It's *Mon*day. This is one of my days off from school and look how I'm spending it."

"Yeah, some vacation," grumbled Haley. She sat up and brushed leaves out of her hair, but she missed one. It was sitting on top of her head.

Becca burst into giggles. She pointed at Haley's head. But Haley's only response was to swat the leaf angrily away.

Jeff, who had rarely complained since we landed on "Nine O'Clock Island," now said, "And besides missing my vacation, I'm freezing. This cave is like a refrigerator."

"I'll add some stuff to the fire," I told him quickly.

"Add our bed," grumbled Jeff. "It's useless. We might as well be sleeping on the floor. The leaves don't do a thing."

"I will *not* add your bed to the fire," I told him. "Maybe we can figure out a way to make it more comfortable."

That made Becca start to cry.

"What's wrong?" I asked her. I put my arm across her shoulder.

"You mean we're still going to be here to-*night*? We're going to need this bed *again*?"

Oops. "No," I answered. "I mean, maybe. We don't know. But just in case."

Becca nodded, sniffling.

"Well, who's hungry?" I asked.

Of course, Becca, Haley, and I were starving. We hadn't eaten since our lunchtime candy bars. Worse than that, we were thirsty.

"Couldn't we have just a *little* of Jamie's water?" begged Haley.

"I'd like to let you have some, but it's gone," I told her. "He finished it a couple of hours ago. For what it's worth, he seems better."

Becca actually began to wring her hands. "But what are we going to drink? People need liquids. I know that from science class. And the juice boxes and *every*thing are gone!"

"I know. I thought about that."

"Can we drink ocean water?" asked Haley.

"Absolutely not," I told her. "It's full of salt. But we can collect rainwater. Look outside. It's going to storm again."

"What will we collect it in?" asked Becca sensibly.

"Can you really drink rainwater?" asked Haley.

"Sure you can drink it. And you can collect it in, um, in . . ."

"We'll rig up something," Jeff said.

"Oh, wait a sec. We aren't thinking!" exclaimed Haley. "We can drink coconut milk! I've seen that in lots of movies. All you do is climb the coconut tree, pick the coconut, punch holes in the end, and there you go. Coconut milk to drink. I think that would be better than rainwater."

I glanced at Jeff, who shrugged. Finally I said, "Haley, this — this isn't a desert island. There are no coconuts in Connecticut. I promise you."

"But there might be coconut trees on *this*

island. We don't know where we are. Can Becca and I please, please, please go get some coconuts?''

"Well . . . all right. But stay around here. Try to keep the cave in sight. And don't go near the water. And for heaven's sake come back if you get too cold. We don't want any other patients on our hands."

"Okay!" The girls ran off excitedly.

Jeff and I grinned at each other.

"Well, *I'm* going fishing," said Jeff. "I'll try to catch a whole lot of fish. You know Becca and Haley won't find any coconuts, and they might just be hungry enough to eat some fish."

"Even *I* might eat fish," I said, my stomach rumbling. "As long as I don't have to look at them first."

"I'll cover their heads," said Jeff as he set off.

The cave was quiet for the next hour. Dawn and Jamie slept. I got bored. Very bored. And worried. How *were* we going to get rescued? And where were we? How far could we have drifted? Were we off the coast of Massachusetts now? Or New York? Or were we way out to sea? I had no idea which direction the storm had blown us. If only the weather would clear. That would help the searchers *and* us. On the other hand, we needed the rain for drinking water.

Rain! I better think of some way to collect it.

Now what would hold water? I looked over our few possessions. Only the plastic tarps seemed like good possibilities. But they were flat. We needed a container. And then I had an idea. (I felt like Kristy, who is always getting good ideas.) I left the cave, found four sturdy sticks, stuck them in the sand in front of the cave, and tied one corner of a tarp to each stick. The tarp sagged nicely in the middle. It would hold plenty of water.

I was quite pleased with myself, since I am not noted for my problem-solving abilities.

When I returned to the cave, Dawn was awake.

"What's going on?" she asked, sitting up.

I told her about my rain-catching idea, and that Jeff was out fishing and the girls were out looking for coconuts.

Dawn smiled. Then she leaned over, peered at Jamie, and felt his forehead. "Well, he seems better," she said.

"I know."

At that moment, we heard the patter of rain outside the cave. In moments, Becca, Haley, and Jeff all reappeared. They were wet and chilly, and the girls, of course, had not found any coconuts. But Jeff was carrying quite a few fish.

"Good job!" I said to him. Then I added cheerfully, "Is everyone ready for a fish fry this morning?"

The girls looked dubious. "Are *you* going to eat fish?" Becca asked me.

"I sure am. As long as I don't have to look — Jeff, keep those things away from me!" I cried, as Jeff teased me with the fish.

Jeff and Dawn prepared the fish, and I looked out the cave entrance at my water collector. "It's working!" I announced. "We'll have water — as long as the tarp doesn't get too full and collapse the sticks."

A little while later, every one of us except Jamie sat down to a breakfast of fish. The girls picked at it at first, but soon they were eating hungrily. I was, too.

"You know," said Becca, "this isn't so bad. It tastes a little like . . ."

"Chicken?" suggested Haley.

"No. I guess it just tastes like fish."

"Well, when you're *really* hungry, anything will do," I said.

"Even rattlesnake meat?" asked Jeff.

"No, I would draw the line there."

"Grubs?" asked Becca.

"No!" I cried. I was glad to see everyone laughing, though. We were more apt to pull through this thing if we kept our spirits up.

By the time breakfast was over, the sun was peeking through the clouds, and Jeff, Becca, and Haley ventured outside again. When they were gone, Dawn and I looked at each other. Dawn was frowning.

"What's wrong?" I asked her.

"The kids may be in good moods," she said, "but you do realize that we're in a critical situation, don't you? I mean, we can't live on fish and rainwater forever. And Jamie needs a doctor."

"I know," I said. I let out a breath I didn't even know I'd been holding.

"How far from Stoneybrook do you think we are?"

"I just don't have any idea. And," I went on, anticipating her next question, "I don't know if they're still searching for us. They probably think we've all drowned."

"Claudia!"

"Well, they probably do. But that shouldn't prevent us from trying to be rescued. There must be some way to attract attention to ourselves."

"A fire?"

"Too dangerous."

"We could still try to escape. We could build a raft."

"No way," I said.

"Got any better ideas?"

"Nope."

"Well, then, we'll just have to keep thinking."

CHAPTER 17

Stacey

Monday

Dear Dad,
   I'm writing this letter on the train, so I hope you can read my wobbly handwriting. I'm really sorry about our fight. I want you to know that I'm not mad at you. And I want to come back to New York again soon.

   I liked the play on Saturday a lot. But I have to tell you something. I'm upset that you didn't let me come home when I needed to. Plus, I think it is unfair that you and Mom fight over me sometimes. I'm sorry you got divorced, but don't put me in the middle. It isn't any easier being a divorced kid than being a divorced parent. My time should be my time, not yours or Mom's.

Thank you for letting me come home early today, and I'll see you in two weeks. I'll call you as soon as I know what has happened to Dawn and Claud.

LUV,

Your daughter, Stacey

That was one difficult letter to write. I felt as if I were telling off my father, and that's something kids aren't supposed to do. At least, it was something *this* kid isn't supposed to do. I hoped I had said enough nice things in the letter to make up for the not-so-nice things.

I was supposed to stay in New York until five o'clock Monday afternoon, but when I woke up on Monday morning, I knew I couldn't stand it there a second longer. I *had* to get back to Stoneybrook and help search for my friends. I knew they hadn't been found yet because I'd spoken to Kristy on Sunday and I'd said, "If they're found, call me right away, no matter what time it is."

"Even if it's two o'clock in the morning?" Kristy had asked.

"Even then. I don't care if the phone *does* wake up my father."

"We-ell . . ." said Kristy.

"*Please*. Promise me."

"Okay. I promise."

I knew Kristy would keep a promise. And she hadn't called me. Plus, I hadn't seen anything about a rescue on the news.

That does it, I thought, when I woke up at seven-thirty on Sunday. I'm going home as soon as I can. No matter what Dad says.

Well, of course, Dad didn't like the idea a bit. That was when we had our fight. Dad watched me throwing stuff in my suitcase and he said, "This was supposed to be a three-day weekend, Stacey."

"Oh, and I guess my friends were *supposed* to get lost at sea on this three-day weekend? It's not like they *chose* to get lost just to mess up *your* weekend with me."

"Anastasia!"

"Dad, you are not being fair. If two of your friends were lost — one of them your *best* friend — wouldn't you want to search for them? Or would you just kick back and say, 'Hey, it's my weekend. Don't ruin it.' "

"Young lady — " Dad began. Then he stopped. "You really want to leave?"

"*Yes*. I want to get back to Stoneybrook and help search. Everyone else is helping. I feel like a spoiled brat here in the city, going to plays and eating in restaurants. My friends are — Well, who knows what they're doing. I bet they aren't having fun or eating good food, though."

Dad shrugged. "If you want to go, go."

So I did. I finished packing my suitcase, got into a cab, and rode to the train station. But I felt horrible. I think I'd wanted Dad to say he was sorry. But he hadn't. I was just leaving him all hurt and everything. Of course, I hadn't apologized to him.

So I had written that letter to Dad. I hoped it would help us to make up. As soon as I finished the letter, I tucked it into my backpack to mail later, and tried to forget about New York.

It was time to concentrate on Stoneybrook.

Not much happened during the rest of the ride. I tried to read, but couldn't. I found myself urging the train along instead. Hurry *up*, hurry *up*, hurry *up*, I said in my head to the rhythm of the wheels flying down the tracks.

At last, the train pulled into the Stoneybrook station. I was already standing by the door with my backpack and my suitcase, ready to get off. And that was when I realized something. I hadn't called Mom from New York. She was expecting me around dinnertime that evening.

"Darn," I said, as I stepped onto the platform. This was what I got for fighting with Dad. and —

"Stacey?"

"Mom?" I couldn't believe it! "How did you know I was on this train?" I asked her.

"Your father called me right after you left the apartment."

"Oh. So I guess you know about our fight."

"I know your father's side of it. Come on," said Mom, putting her arm around me and taking the backpack, which I was struggling with. "Why don't you tell me your side on the way home?"

"Can I tell it to you on the way to the community center?" I replied. "I want to go straight there and help search."

"Of course," said Mom. So I told her the story as we drove through town.

"I wrote him a letter," I added, as we arrived at the center.

Mom parked the car, but neither of us got out.

"Do you want to tell me about the letter?" asked my mother.

"I'll do better than that," I said. "You can read it." I searched through my backpack for the book I'd stuck the letter in. "Here it is." I handed it to Mom. Mom read it and sighed.

"What? Are you mad at me, too?" I asked.

"No," said Mom, but she bent her head over and rested it on her fingertips like she does sometimes when she's angry.

"You are! You are mad!" I exclaimed.

And some stupid WATL reporter chose *that moment* to stick her microphone through the car window and ask, "Friends of the missing?"

I was stunned. Since I'd been away for the weekend, I had no idea what was going on at the community center. Now I took a look around. The parking lot was overflowing. Mom wasn't even parked in an actual space, because there weren't any. She'd just pulled up near the door to the center. I saw a couple of WATL vans, a helicopter hovering over the beach near the dock, and a lot of boats.

"What?" I said, searching the face of the reporter. "Are we friends of the missing?"

"Yes," said the reporter.

"I am," I replied.

"Well, how do you *feel*, knowing that your friends are gone?"

"I feel terrible!" I cried. "What did you expect? I feel — "

Mom cut me short. She put an end to the interview by hitting the button that makes all the windows in the car roll up. The reporter had to act quickly to get her microphone out

before it got squished by the window.

"Mom!" I exclaimed. Then I paused. "Thanks," I said.

We both began to laugh.

"Honey," said my mother, "I'm not angry. Really I'm not. At least not with you. I think I'm angry at myself, though. And maybe at your father. We don't mean to put you in the middle of things, but if we do . . . then we should stop. I promise we'll try harder."

"Thanks," I said. I looked out the window. "Whoa. I wonder what's going on." There was a flurry of activity among the news reporters. They were all running for the center. "Maybe there's some news!" I exclaimed. "Come on, Mom!"

We dashed inside, even though our car wasn't properly parked. And the first person I saw in that crowded room was Kristy.

"Stacey!" she cried.

"Kristy!"

We hugged quickly.

Then I said, "What happened? What's going on?" at the same time that *Kristy* said, "You're home early!"

"I know. I'll explain later," I told her. "But what *is* this?"

Kristy sighed. "I don't know what to make of this news, but one of the search boats found

Stacey

an empty sailboat early this morning. It's Claudia's. They checked the numbers on the boat. There's no question about it. The boat is in good condition, but it's completely empty. I mean, even the food and supplies are missing.''

"An empty boat," I repeated slowly.

Kristy nodded.

"No hole or anything?"

"Nope. It was just floating along."

At that point we heard a newscaster say to a tired-looking searcher, "You say there were no signs of a struggle on board?"

"A *struggle?*" said Kristy. "What do they think happened? That pirates raided the sailboat?" Kristy looked furious.

"Never mind," I said to her.

"Hey, you guys!"

Mallory ran up to us then.

"We heard the news," said Kristy before Mallory could go on.

"Well, what are we waiting for?" said Mal. "Mom and Dad and the triplets and Nicky and Vanessa are here. We're ready to go searching again. Who wants to come with us?"

I don't know why, exactly, but for some reason, instead of answering Mal, I burst into tears.

"Stacey?" said my mother from behind me.

"They found one of the sailboats this morning," I said sort of hysterically. "It was empty. That can't be a good sign!"

"Oh, Stace," said Mom. "Come on. Let's go home."

I almost went with her. But at the last moment I turned around. "Wait," I said. "I want to search after all. That's why I came home, isn't it? To search?"

"How many times have you been out on a boat?" Mom wanted to know. "Other than a cruise ship."

"Almost none. But I *have* to go. And Mal says they have room for me."

"We-ell . . ."

Mom had softened. "See you later!" I called to her.

I ran back to Kristy and Mallory and the rest of the Pikes. "Is there still room for me?" I asked.

"Of course," said Mrs. Pike. "Okay, everybody. Let's get ready."

CHAPTER 18

Mallory

Monday

My journal sure has gotten full the last few days. I'm sorry that it had to become full because of a tragedy but, in a way, I like having a record of the mystery and the search. I wonder if that's morbid. No. I have a feeling that someday this will be useful or meaningful to someone.

Today we went looking for our lost friends again. We've spent so much time on the water that whenever I close my eyes now, all I see is an endless blue-green expanse. And I can feel the boat rocking under me. At least today's search was different from yesterday's. I don't know if it was better, though. Just different. What made it different was that on today's search, we actually found something . . . .

Monday morning started early, unlike most vacation days. By seven o'clock, I could hear Mom and Dad rustling around in the kitchen. Even though they had said the night before that we wouldn't go out on any boats today until late in the morning or even lunchtime, I joined them for an early breakfast. I like spending quiet time alone with Mom and Dad.

But by eleven-thirty that morning my family, except for Claire and Margo, who stayed behind with Mary Anne, had gathered at the community center, ready for another day of boating and searching. We met up with Kristy and Stacey at the center. They wanted to come with us, especially since there was finally some news: Claudia's boat had been found. It was in perfect condition — but empty.

"I don't get it," I said to Dad. "What could that mean?"

Dad was frowning. "I don't know. That's a real mystery."

"The food and supplies are gone," I said thoughtfully. "Maybe it's a good sign. How could those things just disappear from the boat? They had to have been taken off. Some of them are stored under the seats."

"That's a good point," said Dad.

The reporters, of course, were terribly excited by the news. They picked it up and shook it like a dog with a rabbit, and wouldn't let it go.

They made everyone crazy.

Dad wanted to get us organized and on boats again. He called all of us — our family, Kristy, and Stacey — together on the dock behind the center.

"Since there are so many of us, we'll take two big boats out today. We'll divide up like this: Kristy, Stacey, Mal, and Jordan with me. The rest of you with your mom."

Of course, Kristy and Stacey and I liked this arrangement fine. We *wanted* to be together. Unfortunately, so did the triplets — Jordan, Adam, and Byron. They did *not* want to be split up, but they didn't have a say in the matter.

"Life preservers, everyone," announced Dad.

We separated, stepped onto the boats, and put on life preservers.

Our second day of searching had begun.

We left the dock behind us and headed into Long Island Sound.

"Which direction are we going in?" I asked Dad. "Back to Greenpoint again?"

"I think we'll go east of there," he replied. "The empty boat was found several miles to the east."

"Okay."

Dad steered the boat, and Stacey, Kristy, and Jordan and I hung over the sides, looking, looking, looking.

"What are we looking *for?*" asked Stacey.

"Anything unusual," said Dad.

"Hey!" said Jordan. "I have an idea. Let's bear east but let's go there by way of all the little islands. We can go out to Greenpoint and then go east. That way, if they landed on one of the islands, we can see them and rescue them."

(Jordan desperately wanted to be a hero.)

"Well," said Dad, "okay. That'll take a long time to do, but it's a good idea."

I imagined us passing an island and hearing cries.

"Help! Here we are! Rescue us!"

Hmmm. Maybe it would be fun to be heroes.

So we headed for Greenpoint and soon passed it. We didn't talk much as we moved. We just looked and looked and looked at the water and the islands. The water was as smooth as glass, and the color of an emerald. But the sky was still hazy and . . .

"Look up there," said Kristy.

"What? What do you see?" asked Stacey, swiveling around.

"Oh, sorry," replied Kristy. "I don't see *them*. It's just, well, I think we're in for another storm."

Kristy was pointing to clouds, to looming thunderheads.

"Oh, brother," murmured Jordan.

"How much time do we have?" I asked Dad. "When do we have to turn around?"

"Now," my father answered. "We don't want to get caught in *that* storm."

"Why can't the weather clear *up?*" I cried. I nearly stamped my foot. I was so frustrated. "We'll never find anything this way. Not if we have to keep turning the boat around and coming in."

Nobody answered me. They knew the weather was something we just had to put up with.

"Uh-oh," said Stacey suddenly. "Mr. Pike, what if Mrs. Pike didn't see the storm clouds? What if they aren't coming in?"

"They're coming," my dad answered. "I just spoke to Adam on the radio."

"Where are they, anyway?" wondered Stacey. "I lost sight of them."

"They're a little ahead of us, but not this far east," said Jordan. "Right, Dad?"

"Exactly right."

We had turned around and were heading

back. Jordan and my friends and I continued to scan the water for . . . anything.

We were about halfway back to Stoneybrook when Stacey said, "What's that?"

"What's what?" replied Jordan, who was standing next to her.

"That." Stacey pointed out to the ocean. "Way over there."

Stacey must have eyes like an eagle to see through the haze. I didn't see anything but water.

"Mr. Pike," said Stacey, "I see something floating over there. Honest. Can we head just a little closer to it?"

Dad looked at the sky and then at his watch. "Okay," he said. "Here we go."

We headed east slightly. Soon even I could see something in the water. But we weren't sure what it was until we were practically on top of it.

"A piece of wood," said Kristy.

"Hey, there's another one!" shouted Jordan, pointing.

"Do you see any numbers or letters on it?" asked Dad.

"Yes," said Stacey right away, not knowing why my father was asking. "I see a two, a three, and maybe part of a five."

Dad looked grim.

"It's from Dawn's boat, isn't it?" I said. My voice had dropped to a whisper.

"From Dawn's boat?" repeated Stace. "What do you mean?"

"We know what to look for," said Dad gently. "The numbers on the boats are what identify them."

"And the number on Dawn's boat had a two-three-five in it?" asked Stacey.

"Yes," replied Dad.

"But . . . it can't — I mean, that boat is in pieces. It's all broken up. I can see several more . . ." Stacey trailed off.

Dad put us back on course to Stoneybrook again.

"Wait!" cried Stacey. "We can't turn around now."

"We have to," spoke up Kristy, who'd been awfully quiet. "We have to beat the storm back. And we have to report what we found. Don't worry, th — "

Stacey cut her off. Just barely holding back tears, she cried, "Don't *worry*? You're as bad as my father. Claudia and the others are . . . well, who knows where they are. Obviously, they're not on either of the boats. And think of all the stuff that's out here waiting to get them. There could be sharks, sea snakes, jellyfish. Not to mention these storms we keep having."

Kristy put her arm around Stacey. I wanted to do the same thing, since Stacey had started to cry. However, now I had started to cry, too.

Jordan didn't know what to make of the situation. He was as startled by the discovery of the bits of boat as we were, and he was worried about Jeff, who's his friend, but he gave my father a look that plainly said, "*Girls.*"

Dad didn't notice. Yelling over the wind that was starting to pick up, he said, "I really don't think you need to worry about sharks or sea snakes, girls. Trust me."

"Okay, what about drowning?" Stacey yelled back.

No one had an answer for that.

We sailed back to the community center in silence, unless you count the blustery wind that roared in our ears. We reached the center just after Mom and the others — and just as the rain began. The boats were barely docked when fat raindrops started to fall from the sky, and thunder rumbled. We dashed into the center, where Dad made a report about what we'd found.

Naturally, this caused the newscasters and reporters to become nearly maniacal, especially when they noticed that Kristy, Stacey, and I were all in tears.

We were rescued from their questions, though. Both Mrs. McGill and Charlie Thomas were at the center, so they drove Stacey and Kristy to their homes. Then my family and I went back to our house, where Mom actually put me to bed and made me some tea. I don't remember the last time I was so upset.

Soon, though, feeling better, I phoned Stacey. We talked about everything except the awful pieces of wood.

"Do you think school will be open tomorrow?" Stacey wondered.

"I don't know," I replied. "Everyone is searching. Half the teachers from SMS have been combing the beach."

When Stacey and I hung up, I just sat on Mom and Dad's bed. I didn't know what to do.

I felt completely helpless.

CHAPTER 19

Claudia

Looking Back—
Late Mondy Mornig and
Early Mondy Afternon
I was sick and tried of of all those
long faces everyone was just mopping
around and it was making me crazy.
I decided to do somthing about it. So
I left dawn watching jamie and I
left Jeff watching the girls and I went
into the woods to see what I could find....

My water collection idea had worked pretty well, but just after breakfast we discovered something: You couldn't leave it alone too long, especially if the rain was coming down hard.

Becca and Haley were cleaning up after our breakfast, which meant collecting the fish bones and dumping them outside the cave. (We figured that they were "natural" garbage and would disintegrate, unlike the rest of our trash.)

"Besides," said Becca, working hastily, "we don't want the cave to smell like fish." Then she added, "Not that the fish was bad, Jeff."

Jeff grinned. He knew that Becca and Haley and I had eaten the fish out of desperation, but he didn't mind.

Becca had just run out of the cave with her pile of fish bones when the rest of us heard her exclaim, "Uh-oh!"

"What-oh?" asked Haley.

"Everybody get out here *quick!*" cried Becca.

Jeff and Haley and I joined her, but Dawn stayed behind with Jamie. Nobody had to ask Becca what the problem was. We could see it clearly. The water collector was full and about to collapse.

"Quick! You guys hold tight to the posts.

Don't let them cave in!" I yelled. Then I dashed inside and gathered up every empty container I could find. When I ran back out, I saw Jeff, Haley, and Becca each straining to hold up a stick. The fourth pole was about to cave in.

As quickly as I could, I submerged each bottle in the water, filled it to the brim, and set it on the ground. I was almost finished when . . . *whoosh, crash!* That fourth pole collapsed and the rest of the water splashed to the ground.

"Darn!" cried Jeff. "All that wasted water."

"Well, it could be worse," said Haley philosophically. "At least we have *some* water. And it'll probably storm again soon. Then we can collect more."

"That's true," I said. "Come on, you guys. Help me set everything up again. We might as well be prepared."

The kids and I righted the poles and tied the tarp to them again. Then we examined our water supply.

"I guess it's not the most sanitary in the world," I said, thinking that every bottle had been drunk out of by someone else, and that the water hadn't been purified, and I wasn't sure how clean the tarp had been. "But it's better than nothing."

"I'll say," agreed Haley. She picked up a juice box that we'd torn the top off of, and drank thirstily. "Not bad," she remarked, after she'd downed half of it.

"Okay, go slowly everybody," I warned them. "Jamie will need some of this water, and we should make the rest of it last as long as we can."

The kids helped me bring the water into the cave. I carried a bottle over to Jamie. "How's he doing?" I asked Dawn.

Dawn's face was as long as — as I'm not sure what. She looked awful.

"Not so well," she replied. "I think his fever's up again. And I've been wondering. Do you think we should wake him up to feed him?"

"Feed him *fish?*" I said, horrified. "He'd never forgive us."

"I'm serious. He hasn't eaten since lunch yesterday, and that was just a candy bar. Maybe he needs food to help him fight whatever he's got."

"I don't know. I wouldn't wake him up just to feed him. But if he wakes up on his own and says he's hungry, then Jeff can go fishing again. Meanwhile, here's more water."

"Oh, good," said Dawn. "I *am* going to wake him up for a drink. His fever was down

174

as long as he was having water."

So Dawn and I roused the sleeping Jamie.

"We've got more water," Dawn told him.

I helped her raise Jamie into a sitting position. Jamie drank for a long time. Then he fell asleep again.

"Claudia, can we go to the beach?" asked Haley, not looking terribly enthusiastic about the idea. "All of us?" Then she added dramatically, "The air is thick with germs."

"Sure. I'll come with you. Or maybe Dawn will." I turned to Dawn. "Want to take a break and go to the beach?"

Dawn shook her head. "I'll stay here with the germs." She was trying to be funny, but she looked like she was going to cry any second.

"All right," I said hesitantly.

I walked the kids outside. Their faces now looked about as long as Dawn's. I was pretty sure that what with the excitement of breakfast and water-collecting being over, their worries were setting in again. Plus, they were bored with the beach. That came through loud and clear.

We reached the edge of the water and the kids plopped down and just sat there. They didn't even talk. After a few minutes I couldn't take it anymore. I had to *do* something.

175

"All right," I said, "I'm going to take a little walk. Jeff, you're in charge. Dawn's back in the cave if you have any problems. Stay out of the water and don't go anywhere without telling Dawn." Before they could ask questions, I took off. I marched into the woods.

How, I wondered, could we attract attention to ourselves so we could be rescued? Becca had been right in trying to draw the attention of people in planes, but the shells were not going to work. What else could be seen from a plane? I looked all around me. I saw trees and shrubs and some flowers I didn't recognize. I saw poison ivy and avoided it. I noticed logs and leaves and branches and insects.

And then I saw something bright on the ground. What was it? I bent down and picked up a broken piece of . . . glass? No, I could see myself in it. It was a piece of mirror. It was big, and the edges were jagged. I had to hold it carefully. I didn't know how it had found its way to the island, but I knew what to do with it.

I raced out of the woods, along the beach to the cave, and inside the cave to Dawn, who was dozing next to Jamie.

I shook her shoulder. "Look what I found!" I said in an excited whisper.

"What?" Dawn sat up dazedly.

"A mirror, that's what."

"Big deal. And where have you *been?* I looked outside before and I couldn't see you. Just Jeff and Becca and Haley."

Ooh, touchy. I ignored Dawn's outburst. "Don't you know what we can do with this?" I asked her. "If we wash it off, we can use it to signal planes. Seriously. *I* saw it from up above because it was in a little patch of sun. If I saw it, maybe a plane could see it — if the haze ever burns off. We just have to learn how to angle it to catch the sun. I think."

"We-ell," said Dawn dubiously.

"Look, we don't have any better ideas," I told her. "And it will give the kids something to do, um, as soon as this next storm blows over."

I had just noticed how dark the sky was, so I herded Haley, Becca, and Jeff back inside. We waited out the brief rain shower, filled empty containers, and cheered because the water collector didn't collapse.

And then . . . and then . . . we noticed something. The sky had become as clear as a bell! We ran to the beach with our prize, the mirror.

"I want to wash it!" cried Haley, dashing to the ocean.

"Okay, but be careful. It has sharp edges," I told her.

Haley washed the mirror as if she were washing a bomb. Then she dried it on her shirt and handed it to me.

"Beautiful," I told her. I looked at the sky. "Now let's just hope the sun stays out."

"And that a plane flies overhead," Jeff pointed out.

That was true. In the meantime, we experimented. The sun did stay out and the four of us stood on the beach and practiced trying to catch its rays.

Once, Becca did, and she nearly blinded us with the glare.

"It's kind of like calling Batman!" she exclaimed.

We laughed.

I was glad that the kids seemed hopeful again, but I knew that what we were trying to do had only a slim chance of working. We hadn't seen a plane all day.

Still, you never knew.

"Come save us, Batman!" cried Haley.

CHAPTER 20

Kristy

Sunday Morning's
Emergency Meeting
(continued)

Bart was not at all pleased when I called to tell him that I was canceling Monday's game. He just didn't understand. He felt bad about the boating accident but, he wondered, what could I do? Before I could answer his question, he rushed ahead. He said... Well, he said some pretty mean things. But they don't belong in notes from an emergency meeting.

When I picked up the phone that Sunday to call Bart, I was half hoping he wouldn't be there. Unfortunately, Bart himself answered the phone.

"Hello?" he said.

I knew it was Bart's voice. "Hi," I replied. "It's me, Kristy."

I was using the Pikes' upstairs phone and hoped that no one was listening to my call.

"Hi!" Bart sounded glad to hear from me. That would wear off soon. "What's up?" he asked. Then he rushed on, "Oh, any news of your friends?"

"No. That's why I'm calling. Bart, I want to go out searching with the Pikes today, which means I won't be able to hold practice for the Krushers. Besides, half the kids on the team are either searching or down at the community center waiting for news, so they couldn't come anyway. I've got to call off our game tomorrow. We can't hold it if we don't practice." What I didn't add was that if my friends hadn't been found by tomorrow then we'd probably go out searching again anyway. But I didn't want to think about that.

There was silence at Bart's end of the phone.

"Bart?" I said.

"Yeah?"

"Did you hear me?"

"I heard you."

"So our game's off. I'm sorry. We'll have to reschedule it."

"Kristy, I think this is pretty irresponsible of you. We've had the game lined up for weeks. You're going to disappoint a lot of kids."

I was stuck back on the word "irresponsible." I cleared my throat. "Excuse me? You think I'm being irresponsible? Because I want to help search for six missing people, two of whom are very close friends of mine, one of whom is a Krusher, and another of whom is a Krusher cheerleader? I'm a little confused. I'm missing the 'irresponsibility' part."

"Don't be sarcastic, Kristy."

"Me? Sar*cas*tic?"

"Look, I know your team probably isn't ready for the game tomorrow, but that's no reason to cancel it."

"Is that what you think I'm trying to do? Worm my way out of the game?"

"Well — "

"Come on. Tell me. I can take it."

"Okay. Yes, that is what I think you're doing. Your team hasn't beaten mine yet. I think you just don't want to see the Krushers disappointed ag — "

Bart got cut off when I hung up on him.

That was Sunday morning. By early Monday afternoon I hadn't heard from him, although I guess I hadn't really expected to. I mean, *I had* hung up on him. Maybe that was childish, but Bart was being pretty childish himself. What was wrong with him? Hadn't he ever had an emergency before?

Furthermore, didn't he realize that he was making a miserable weekend even more miserable? How dare he pick a fight with me when six people I liked a lot were *missing?*

I soon found that after that awful phone call, Bart was always on my mind. Or at least at the back of my mind. He was there when the Pikes and I went out searching on Sunday afternoon. He was there all evening as I watched the stupid WATL coverage of the *Connecticut Disaster*, waiting for news that didn't come. He was there the next day when the empty boat was discovered, and later when Stacey spotted the pieces of what was probably Dawn's boat.

Would I, I wondered as Charlie drove me home from the center on Monday, ever speak to Bart again? Would the Krushers ever play Bart's Bashers again, or had I ruined that?

I had no idea, and no extra energy to try to figure it out.

While Charlie was still parking the car at our house, I ran inside, crying. I still couldn't get over the fact that we'd found actual *wreckage* of one of the boats.

"Kristy?" said Mom. She was surprised to see me in tears. "What's the matter?" She paused. Then she put her hand to her mouth. "Oh, no," she whispered. "It's bad news, isn't it?"

"No," I said quickly, brushing away my tears. "It isn't that. But Stacey found *pieces* of Dawn's boat."

"Are you sure it was Dawn's boat?" asked Watson, my stepfather. The three of us sat down in the living room. Soon Charlie joined us.

"Well, pretty sure," I answered. "Stacey saw numbers on one piece of wood, and they were three of the numbers on Dawn's boat. In the right order," I added.

"But not the whole number?" said Watson.

"Noooo," I replied slowly.

"Then you can't be sure it was Dawn's boat," Watson pointed out sensibly.

"That's true." I felt just a smidge better. Then Bart crept into my mind and I felt lousy again.

At that moment the phone rang. I know this is awful, but my first thought was, I hope it's

Bart. That was foolish, though. Things almost never work out the way you think they will.

"I'll get it!" I cried anyway. I jumped up.

Watson put his hand out. "Resume yourself," he said, which means, "Sit down." He smiled. "Karen's getting it, I'm sure." (Karen and Andrew were spending the long weekend with us.) "Karen can't get enough of the phone these days."

I listened, but the phone didn't ring again. A few seconds later, Karen bounced into the living room, calling, "Are you here, Kristy?"

"Yup. Is it for me?" I got to my feet.

"Mm-hmm." Karen was grinning.

"Why are you smiling?"

"Because . . ." (Karen ran to me, and tugged at me. I leaned over.) "It's your boyfriend! You told me not to announce that anymore," she added.

So it was Bart after all.

I flew to the extension in Mom and Watson's bedroom, which is the most private extension, calling for Karen to hang up in the kitchen.

"Bart?" I said breathlessly.

"Hi, Kristy." Bart sounded funny. Kind of depressed or something.

"Are you okay?" I asked.

"Yeah. It's just that I've been watching WATL for hours now and I feel terrible about our phone conversation yesterday. I guess, um, I guess I want to apologize. I mean, I *do* want to apologize. I'm sorry."

"That's okay. I'm sorry I hung up on you."

"That's okay."

There was a silence. Finally Bart said, "Maybe this isn't the right time to tell you this, so stop me if you don't want to hear it, but I really feel like I have to say something."

"Okay." Oh, no. What was he going to say? Was he dumping me?

"The thing is," Bart began, "you exaggerate sometimes."

I burst out laughing. "No kidding!" Then I added, "Sorry. It's just that I know I have a big mouth. I'm always getting in trouble because of it."

"Okay. But, see, I can't always tell when you're being straightforward and when you're exaggerating. It would help me a lot if — "

"I won't cry wolf anymore," I told him. "That's a promise."

"Thank you." Bart sounded as relieved as I felt. Then he said, "Listen, I want to help search, if there's anything I can do. And once your friends are found — and I know they will be — *then* we'll talk about rescheduling our game. Is that okay with you?"

Was it okay with me? Of course. In fact, it was great!

"Do you want to go to the community center — ?"

Bart was interrupted by some strange clicks on the phone. At first I thought Karen was eavesdropping on us. I was about to let her have it, when a voice came on the line:

"This is the operator. Is Kristy Thomas there? I have an emergency call for her from a Jessi Ramsey."

"This is Kristy!" I said excitedly. Wow. I had never gotten an *emergency* call.

"Kristy," said the operator, "please have your party hang up so you can talk to Jessi."

"Okay," I replied. "Bart?"

"I'll talk to you later," he said instantly. He hung up.

And then Jessi was on the line. "Kristy! Kristy! I can't talk long, but the community center just called here to say that they've been found. All of them. And they're alive! They're on a little island way up the coast."

I couldn't believe it. I was afraid to believe it. But that didn't prevent me from spreading the news to everyone I could think of.

187

CHAPTER 21

Claudia

Looking Back—
Monday Afternoon

The miror worked! It relly did!
How many grate ideas can I get?
Frist the water colecter and now the
plane singal. Mabe I should become
an inventor insted of a artist I
would probably make more money.

Anyway it was relly funny the
kids were calling for batman. They
were just playing arond yelling, Come
get us batman! Here we are! And
here is are bat singal! Please come
reskew us.

And out of nowhere help arrived....

"Batman! Here we are, Batman!" yelled Becca.

"Yeah, here's our bat signal!" shouted Haley, expertly aiming the mirror at the sun.

"Hey! What's that?" exclaimed Jeff. "Be quiet, you guys," he said impatiently to Haley and Becca.

"What is it?" I asked him.

"SHHH," hissed Jeff. "Just listen."

The four of us stopped and listened.

And we heard a plane.

"An airplane, an airplane! Oh, my lord, an *air*plane!" I shrieked.

"Where is it?" asked Haley.

The four of us craned our necks back. Haley was still holding the mirror.

"There it is!" I cried. "Haley, aim the mirror! Aim it at the plane."

"I'll do it!" said Jeff.

"No, I will!" We were all grabbing for the mirror.

"Well, *some*body do it — quick!" shouted Becca. She was jumping up and down, waving her arms frantically.

In the end, I was the one who held the mirror and aimed. "I just hope they can see that," I muttered.

And they could! The plane continued to fly

straight ahead. Then slowly it circled back over the island and flew lower . . . and lower. It dipped its wings.

Jeff, Haley, Becca, and I were screaming and running around. We stopped when the plane dipped its wings, though. We'd never seen a plane do that.

Then we heard a voice from the sky. "This is a search plane!"

"Aughh! It *is* Batman!" shrieked Becca.

"Shh. No, it isn't," I told her.

"Wave your arms if you are Claudia or Dawn." The voice was deep. It was coming over a bullhorn.

I waved my arms.

"Wave again to let us know if you are all on the island."

I waved.

"And wave again if you need a doctor."

I waved.

"Okay. We'll send a Coast Guard ship to you as fast as we can. It will come equipped with food, water, a doctor, and your parents."

"And some Ring-Dings!" I hollered back, but I'm sure the pilot (or whoever was yelling) couldn't hear me.

Another dip of the wings, and the plane headed off in the direction from which it had come.

190

"We're saved! Oh, my lord, we're saved!"
I cried.

"Finally," said Jeff.

"Yeah, it took them long enough," added
Haley.

We looked at her and began to laugh.

"Come on. We've got to tell Dawn," I said.
"We'll have to get Jamie ready to go, and put
out our fire, and you guys make sure we have
all our stuff with us. I don't want anyone getting home and complaining, 'Claudia, I left
my T-shirt on the island.' "

We ran back to the cave in high spirits.

"Dawn! Dawn! The mirror worked!" Becca
cried as soon as we reached the cave entrance.
"A plane flew over and a man is sending a
boat and our parents will be on it!"

"Quit kidding," said Dawn sulkily.

"She isn't kidding," I said. "It just happened. Didn't you hear the guy on the bullhorn?"

"No," replied Dawn. Then she added, "You
aren't kidding, are you? That would be much
too mean."

"It's the truth. Batman's honor," Jeff told
his sister.

Dawn jumped up then and hugged first
her brother, then me. And soon we were all
hugging, except for Jamie. But a few minutes

later, he woke up; groggily, though.

"What are you doing?" he mumbled.

"Celebrating!" replied Dawn. "We're going to be rescued. A plane saw us and a ship will be on its way. Your mommy and daddy will be on the ship."

"A doctor, too," I added. "I'm sure he — "

"Or she — " chimed in Haley.

" — will help you to start feeling better right away."

"Goody," said Jamie, and he fell asleep again.

The wait for the Coast Guard boat seemed endless. Actually, it did take a couple of hours to reach us. But it seemed more like a couple of days. While we waited, we gathered up our belongings. (That took about five minutes.) We decided, though, not to put out our fire or take down our water collector until the Coast Guard ship had actually arrived. We had learned the hard way that you never know what to expect.

Dawn and I were in the cave watching Jamie, whose breathing had become sort of funny, and the kids were outside near the cave entrance, when Jeff shouted, "I see it! I think I see it!"

I was on my feet in a flash. Sure enough, way off in the distance was what looked like a boat. Becca, Haley, Jeff, and I ran to the water's edge and began screaming and waving our arms again. We were afraid the ship would pass us by.

It didn't, though. But since it was huge (well, big) it had to dock offshore. A smaller boat was lowered into the water and a couple of men and a woman were sent to meet us. I guessed that one of them was the doctor.

You know what was the most frustrating thing about our rescue? We could see our parents on the boat — they were all waving and leaning over the railing so far that I was afraid they'd fall into the water, or tip the boat over — but they couldn't come to us and we couldn't go to them. At least, not yet. The doctor would probably check Jamie first, and then we'd go out to the ship on lifeboats. All we could do was wave.

When that first lifeboat came ashore, a man in a sailor's uniform stepped out and waded in to meet us. He and the other man were from the Coast Guard. The woman was the doctor.

"See? I told you," hissed Haley. "The doctor's a woman."

We didn't know those three people from a hole in the wall (as Kristy's stepfather would say) but as soon as they were standing on the beach, we hugged them. I even cried a little,

but they were happy tears. You know what? The three of *them* cried, too.

One of the men even said, "You don't know how glad we are to see you."

"Wrong," I replied. "You don't know how glad *we* are to see *you!*"

Everyone laughed. Then the woman, whose name was Dr. Weber, said briskly, "Now, who needs a doctor? All of you look pretty healthy."

"It's Jamie Newton," I told her. "He's four. He got sick late yesterday afternoon. We're not sure what he's got, but he's running a high fever. Well, it was higher yesterday before we began forcing water on him. And he aches all over, his throat is sore, he has an earache, and now his breathing is funny."

"Okay. I'll take a look at him. He could have a strep throat, or maybe a nice case of the flu. Where is he?"

"In our cave, with Dawn," I replied.

"Yeah, come on," said Becca. "We'll show you."

We walked up the beach with the doctor and the Coast Guard guys.

"There's our water collector," said Jeff, as we approached the cave. "Claudia invented it. It really works."

"Pretty clever," said one of the men. "So you had shelter and water the last couple of days. That's good. What about food?"

"Fish and candy bars," Haley told him, looking disgusted. "I hope you've got good food on your boat."

"Plenty," replied the man. "Water and juice, too."

The four of us sighed with relief — and hunger.

We entered the cave then, introduced Dawn to our rescuers, and let the doctor examine Jamie. The doctor looked sort of concerned, but managed to get some Tylenol into him. Then she said, "The sooner we get him to a hospital the better. Oh," she went on, seeing our stricken faces, "he's not *that* sick, but I need to run a few tests, get his fever down, and just watch him for awhile. He's lucky he had such good care here. You did the right things for him."

Dawn and I smiled.

One of the men picked up Jamie then, Jeff doused our fire with rainwater, we gathered our trash and belongings, and before we knew it, we were standing on the shore, where two more lifeboats had been sent in.

"Good-bye, Nine O'Clock Island," whispered Becca as we were rowed out to the ship.

We were still approaching the ship when the screaming and cheering began.

What a reunion. There have been times when I was so angry at my parents that I wanted to divorce them. But when I finally stepped onto the Coast Guard ship, there were no faces I wanted to see more than Mom's and Dad's.

We hugged practically forever.

And Dawn and Jeff were hugging their mom and stepfather, Becca and Haley were hugging their parents, and Jamie was being fussed over by his parents. I think everybody on board that boat was crying.

And eating. Boy, us castaways set into the food and wolfed it down. While I ate, I tried to tell Mom and Dad about the last 48 hours — how we had wound up on the island and how I, Claudia Kishi, had gotten us off the island. I told them about the water collector, too.

"You know," I finished up, "I *do* promise to study harder in school, but I have to admit, I don't feel nearly so bad about my report card now. I may not be school-smart or book-smart, but I'm practical. I think I'm pretty good at solving problems, aren't I?"

Mom's and Dad's answers? More hugs and tears.

I smiled at them. The boat was halfway to Stoneybrook by then. In a little while we would be back with our friends and brothers and sisters. Home sweet home.

Dawn

Looking Back—
Monday Afternoon

Well.

It's hard to describe our homecoming. It was both the happiest and the most emotional time of my life. Even more emotional (for me) than Mom and Richard's wedding. I guess you just have to have been shipwrecked, washed ashore on an island, and stranded there for two days before you know how it feels to get home and see your family and friends again.

The boat ride to Stoneybrook was pretty incredible, but the reunion at the community center was amazing. Everyone was there— our brothers and sisters, our friends, and... the reporters.

My mother could barely stop hugging Jeff and me as the Coast Guard ship sailed us home. It was as if she couldn't believe we were really safe and alive unless she could touch us. She told us how worried she and Richard had been, and that they'd tried all weekend to get in touch with Dad, but hadn't reached him until just after they received the news that we'd been found.

"Mom?" I said at one point when she'd managed to let go of Jeff, who had run off. "I have to tell you something."

"What is it? This sounds like a confession."

"I guess it is, sort of."

"Okay."

"Well, the thing is, um, the thing is . . ." Mom was watching me seriously. "The thing is, I wasn't much help on the island. I sort of fell apart. I took care of Jamie, but Claudia was the one who did all the thinking. She figured out how to collect rainwater, instead of going without water. And she figured out how to attract attention to ourselves so we could be rescued. She really kept things going."

"Honey, everyone reacts differently in an emergency."

"I know, but I feel like I failed everyone. Or maybe I just feel like I failed myself. I mean, my friends always tell me what a clear head I have. They say I don't let things get me down. But this *did* get me down. I was just another person for Claudia to take care of."

"I don't know, honey," said Mom. "Maybe you didn't come through quite the way you would have expected, but you did know how to nurse Jamie. And I don't think you really fell apart. Let's say the fire in your cave had started burning out of control. Would you have rescued the kids?"

"Of course!"

"If somebody had been injured, would you have tried to give them first aid?"

"Yes."

"Okay. So you didn't fall apart. But maybe you learned something about yourself."

"That I'm a worrier?"

Mom laughed. "No. That you can't always be the strong one. And by not being the strong one for once, I think you helped Claudia learn something about *her*self."

"That she *can* be the strong one? That she can figure out problems?"

"Exactly."

Mom and I hugged. (Again.) I felt much better. Good enough to eat another of the pieces of fruit she'd brought with her.

Not much later I heard a cry: "There it is! There's the dock!"

I turned to look. Sure enough, ahead of us and to our right was the dock and the community center. I almost didn't recognize the dock, though. As we drew closer, I saw why. It was so covered with people that from a distance it looked furry.

"Whoa," I said under my breath.

Soon the ship was docking. First off were the Newtons and Dr. Weber.

The crowd cheered.

Then Mom, Richard, Jeff, and I got off.

More cheering.

What was with all the cameras and reporters? I wondered.

Before I had an answer to my question, I spotted Mary Anne. She and Logan were at the front of the crowd. For the longest time, we just stared at each other. Then Mary Anne held out her arms and I ran to her.

"I promise never to fight with you again!" I cried, at the same time Mary Anne cried, "I'll never stop speaking to you again!"

"Ever?" I asked her. "Even if I forget to give you messages for the rest of my life? Or the rest of your life?"

"Even then."

"Boy," I said. "I ought to get shipwrecked more often."

Mary Anne and Logan and I laughed. And Mary Anne turned to Logan and said, "Do you forgive me? I'm *really* sorry I thought you stood me up. But what else was I supposed to think? We had arranged to meet and you weren't there. I hadn't gotten the message."

"I know, I know, I know," said Logan. "I hope *you'll* forgive me."

"I will," replied Mary Anne.

(Boy. Our rescue was patching up all sorts of arguments.)

I really think Mary Anne and Logan might have kissed right on the dock, but they realized that Mom and Richard were there, not to mention about a zillion people with cameras.

I turned away. I wanted to watch the rest of the castaways have their reunions. Haley had been right behind me. Now she and her brother, Matt, were holding a frantic, happy, sign-language reunion. Since Haley's hands were busier than Matt's, I had a pretty good idea that she was telling about the adventure and how we had survived.

Haley and her parents were followed off the ship by Becca and her parents. I watched Becca fly into the arms of Jessi, who was accompanied by Squirt and some lady I didn't know.

The lady looked a little like Mr. Ramsey, but I'd never seen her before.

"Becca!" Jessi cried.

"Jessi!" Becca cried.

It was right out of a movie.

"You'll never believe this," Becca said, speaking at a pretty fast clip, "but I *ate fish!* I am not kidding."

I laughed. Becca spends two days stranded who-knows-where, and all she can say about her adventure is that she ate fish?

"Hey, Becca," said Jessi, who was laughing, too. "Would you clear something up for me? Would you tell Aunt Cecelia" (Aunt Cecelia?) "who gave you permission to go sailing?"

"Mommy and Daddy did," replied Becca. Then she added, "Aunt Cecelia, how come you're here?"

"It's a long story," Jessi answered before her aunt could open her mouth. Then she said, "See? It really wasn't my fault."

"Hmphh," said Aunt Cecelia. But she gave Jessi a half-smile.

Last off the boat were Claudia and her parents. Claud was greeted by her sister, Janine. They hugged uncomfortably, but looked glad to see each other. I bet Claud couldn't wait to tell the Genius about her water collector and the mirror signal.

"Hey! Hey, Dawn!" yelled a voice.

I looked around. I was in the middle of an enormous, noisy crowd. I saw my brother talking to the Pike triplets. I saw some reporters interviewing parents and scribbling notes on their pads. I saw . . .

Kristy! She was edging through the crowd, followed by Mallory and Stacey. In a flash, all of my friends were together. The hugging continued. So did the tears. Best friends were reunited. The Baby-sitters Club was together again.

"Boy, there were times when I *never* thought this would happen," I said.

"Neither did we," said Kristy, speaking for all the land-bound sitters.

"Yeah, this has been some weekend," added Stacey. "I wanted *so badly* to come back here and search for you, but Dad wouldn't let me leave New York till this morning."

"And Kristy and I have been out searching for you guys," spoke up Mal. "We went out in boats yesterday and today."

"Bart and I had a huge fight about that, believe it or not," added Kristy.

"I *wanted* to search," said Jessi, "but Aunt Cecelia wouldn't let me. She came to stay with Squirt and me when we found out that Becca was gone. Then Mom and Dad came home —

and Aunt Cecelia stayed. She is a pain . . . in
. . . the . . . neck!"

"I wanted to search, too," said Mary Anne,
"but I was basically a basket case over the fight
I'd had with you, Dawn."

That was when I realized that every one of
us BSC members had a different story to tell
about this weekend. It was also when I decided that those stories should be written
down so I would have a record of them.

A news reporter stuck a microphone in my
face then, but I'd barely had time to tell her
my name when the director of the community
center stepped into the crowd with Stoneybrook's mayor.

The director held up his hands. "May I have
your attention, please?"

Flashbulbs flashed. Tape recorders wound
along. TV cameras were rolling.

"Right here," said the director loudly, "we
have two heroes. Dawn Schafer and Claudia
Kishi. They are credited with responsibly car-
ing for four younger children, including Jamie
Newton, whom we have learned is quite ill.
Mayor?"

The mayor pulled Claudia and me next to
her. We stood side by side, as the crowd drew
back a little, leaving us in the center of a circle
of admirers.

"These two young women," said Mayor Keane, "are to be praised for keeping their heads in a difficult, even traumatic, situation."

I think the mayor would have continued speaking, especially since the press was there and she was up for reelection, but Dr. Weber nervously interrupted things.

"I'm sorry," she said, "but I want every one of these kids to come to the hospital now."

"Me?" I exclaimed. "The hospital? Why?"

"I just want you and the others to be checked over. You've had a rough couple of days without much to eat."

"But I'm fine," I protested. "I want to go home."

"I'm sure you'll be able to go home in a couple of hours," Dr. Weber assured me.

Reluctantly, Claud, Becca, Haley, Jeff, and I allowed ourselves to be ushered out of the spotlight to our parents, who were waiting to drive us to the hospital. (Jamie and his parents had gone ahead in an ambulance.)

" 'Bye!" I called to my friends. "I'll talk to you later."

Mom and Richard had to shield Jeff, me, and even Mary Anne from reporters as we left the community center and headed for our car. I felt like a celebrity. But mostly I was glad to be on my way *home*.

CHAPTER 23

The Baby-sitters Club

Friday.

This is our first official post-disaster BSC meeting. Ordinarily, I don't write up regular old meetings, but Dawn wanted me to write this up for some reason. She hasn't said why -- only that she'll tell us later.

Okay, so first of all we missed our Wednesday meeting. Boy, it's been a long time since we missed a meeting. But we had a good reason. And we didn't let our clients down, either. We borrowed the Kishis' answering machine, hooked it up to Claud's phone, and changed the message so that it said: "Hello, you have reached the headquarters of the Baby-sitters Club. We can't come to the phone today, Wednesday, from five-thirty until six, but we'll be back at our post on Friday, as usual. If you want to line up a sitter, please leave your name, number, and a message after the signal, and Claudia will get back to you as soon as possible. Thank you." Then each of us said our names. We had solved the problem pretty well.

Anyway, we didn't conduct a very official meeting on Friday. That was because we were too busy talking about what we'd been doing on Wednesday during club meeting time....

Dawn

Mary Anne didn't know it yet, but the reason I'd asked her to take notes on the meeting was to help me write about our adventure. I wanted a record of the *entire* adventure — from the events leading up to it, to the aftermath. And Friday was pretty much the end of things except, of course, that no club member, especially the two of us who'd been stranded on the island, would ever really be quite the same again.

Friday's meeting began earlier than most other meetings. This was not because Kristy had asked us to arrive early. We just showed up by about 5:15, instead of later. We'd been spending an awful lot of time together since Claud and I had returned.

Mary Anne and I were the first to show up.

"Hi!" we greeted Claudia.

"Hi," she replied. "Have you seen the paper yet?"

"No. Is the story out already?"

"Special edition," said Claud, grinning.

"Where is it?" I shrieked.

"I'm not telling. I'm saving it for the beginning of the meeting."

"Oh, no! You can't! That is too unfair! I will *die* waiting."

"You've only got about fifteen minutes to

go. Anyone who was stranded on an island for forty-eight hours can wait fifteen minutes in my nice, cozy bedroom. Come on. I'll even feed you. I've got plenty of stuff here."

Claud began rummaging around under her bed and in her closet. She emerged with Ring-Dings for herself and Mary Anne, and pretzels for me. "Settle down," she told me.

Easier said than done. Especially when I realized something. "*You've* read the paper already, haven't you?"

"Nope," said Claud.

"Come on. How could you have the article and not read it?"

"I just did, that's all. I saw the headline . . . and I hid the paper."

"Oh, puh-*lease* just tell us what the headline says."

Claudia caved in. "Oh, all right. The headline says: 'Connecticut Disaster Victims Tell Their Story.' "

"Wow," whispered Mary Anne. "That is so dramatic."

A few moments later, Stacey arrived. Then Mal, Jessi, and Kristy showed up. It still wasn't 5:15.

"The article is out!" I announced as each club member arrived.

As soon as Kristy had settled herself in the

director's chair and was wearing her visor, I said, "Okay, Claud. We're all here."

Claudia left the room and returned shortly with the *Stoneybrook News*. "I hid it in Janine's room," she explained.

She spread the paper open on her bed. We had made the *front page*. The letters in the headline were each about two inches tall. They took up half the page. I'd never seen anything like it. And as I read the story, I thought back to how it had come about.

On Monday, after our rescue, we were driven to the hospital. (Well, except for Jamie, who had gone in the ambulance.) We didn't have to stay long. There wasn't much wrong with any of us. Haley had a sunburn, despite the haze and our efforts to keep ourselves gooed up with sunscreen. Jeff had cut his foot and not said anything about it and now the bottom of his foot was slightly infected. We were all somewhat hungry, although no one could say we were starving. We weren't dehydrated, thanks to Claud's rain collector. We *were* tired, both physically and emotionally. To be perfectly honest, none of us smelled that great. And we'd been exposed to Jamie, who had a strep throat in addition to an ear infection, but whether we'd caught anything from him would remain to be seen. (So far, none of us has.)

We were home in time for late dinners with our families that night. (Except, once again, for Jamie, who was spending the night in the hospital, just to be on the safe side.)

The next day was Tuesday. School started again, but the castaways all got to stay home and rest. Jeff was supposed to have flown back to California the night before, but he went back late Tuesday afternoon instead. And early Tuesday afternoon, Jamie came home from the hospital. Claudia, Haley, Becca, Jeff, and I were there to greet him. (Okay, so we didn't rest *that* much.) We were sitting on the Newtons' front porch when their car drove up.

The five of us jumped to our feet.

"Hi, Jamie!" we called. "Welcome home!"

Mrs. Newton, smiling, climbed out of the car, carrying Lucy. I fully expected Mr. Newton to pick up Jamie and carry *him*, but Jamie bounced out of the car, wearing a brand-new outfit, his hair freshly washed and slicked back, and ran to his fellow disaster victims.

"Slow down, Jamie," warned Mr. Newton.

But Jamie was feeling too good to slow down.

"Hi, I'm fine now!" exclaimed Jamie. "My

throat is better and my ear is better and my tempature is almost gone."

"Jamie, you're not com*plete*ly well," spoke up Mrs. Newton. "Remember what the doctors told you?"

"Oh, yeah. To rest and take my medicine. When can I stop resting?"

"When your temperature has been normal for twenty-four hours — one day."

Jamie sighed. "Okay." But then he grinned.

So did we. It's hard to describe the way the six of us felt. Those two days we'd spent on the island had seemed a lot longer, and we were more comfortable together than apart, no matter how much we appreciated being back with our families again.

On Tuesday evening, just after Mom and Richard and I had returned from taking Jeff to the airport, the phone rang.

Richard answered it. He rolled his eyes, cupped his hand over the phone and whispered to us, "Another reporter." But then he said (in his regular voice), "Oh, the *Stoneybrook News*. . . . The mayor? . . . WATL?"

"TV?" I squeaked. "What is it?"

"A press conference," Richard whispered.

Believe it or not, an actual *press* conference was arranged for the next day. Everyone wanted to interview the survivors of the *Connecticut Disaster*, and this seemed like a good way to do it. We would talk to all the reporters and newscasters at once. Besides, Claud and I were *dying* to be on TV, and if we could arrange it, we wanted to get the other members of the BSC on TV and in the papers with us.

We were sorry that Jeff couldn't be here for the press conference, but Jamie was well enough to attend, so that was good. The conference was held at — where else? — the community center. Our families came with us, as well as Kristy, Stacey, and Mal. And Claud and I insisted they stand with our families. We figured we had a little pull.

Boy, was the community center a sight. Just like on Monday, after we were rescued, there were cameras and reporters galore, but since they were crammed into one room, there seemed to be even more of them.

Nearly everyone was interviewed, but the disaster victims did the most talking. The mayor presented all of us with medals of courage. She had one for Jeff, too, which she was going to send him personally. The local news covered our story that night, but they had warned us that they had time for only a five-minute spot. That was pretty exciting, but what we'd all been waiting for was the giant newspaper article (with lots of pictures) that we'd been promised.

We saw it, of course, at our Friday club meeting.

"What does it say? What does it say?" cried Mary Anne. "Do they quote me anywhere? Where's my picture?"

"*Your* picture?" I retorted. "You weren't even on the island." Then I caught myself and added, "Sister dear."

The article was pretty impressive. It took up most of what was left of the front page below the enormous headline. Then it was continued inside. That was where the photos were — a whole page of them. There was a picture of the disaster victims, a picture of Mary Anne and me hugging, and, lo and behold, a picture of the BSC members.

"Ooh," said Stacey. "I know. Let's each cut out this picture from our own copies of the paper, frame the pictures, and hang them in our bedrooms."

"Great idea," said Kristy. "Hey! This article is good advertising for the club!"

Well, by this time it was twenty to six. Kristy hadn't called us to order or anything. We got two job calls, but Mary Anne just hastily lined up sitters. Then we returned to the article.

"I feel like a hero. I mean, a heroine," said Claudia.

"Me, too," I admitted.

"Hey!" exclaimed Claud. "I just thought of something."

"What?" I asked.

"We never finished our sailing race. We're still tied, Schafer. We still need a rematch. How about it?"

I laughed. I knew Claud was kidding. "No way," I told her. "No way."

EPILOGUE

Dawn

And so our island adventure was over -- except that it would never truly be over because I would never forget it. I have written my story using notes from club meetings, diary entries, Stacey's letter to her father, and a lot of notes that Claud' and I made when we got back. I filled in the cracks by interviewing my friends with a tape recorder. Here are final comments from the seven of us:

Claudia — "I never realized that I was smart until I got stuck on that island. Okay, I'm not book-smart like Janine, but I'd rather be practical, anyway. Too bad you don't get graded on practicality in school. Hey, Dawn, I *still* demand a rematch!"

Kristy — "I know I'm no shrinking violet, but I'm glad I stood up for what I believed in last weekend. I'm glad I canceled the Krushers' practice and the game. Searching was more important. But I did learn that when you stand up for yourself, you have to be mature about it.''

Stacey — ''You guys forced me to see that it *is* possible to push parents around. Just kidding. The weekend was . . . I don't know. I realized how tied I am to Stoneybrook now. I grew up in New York, but Stoneybrook is definitely my home. And you guys are part of my family.''

Jessi — ''If Aunt Cecelia stays a second longer I am going to scream. Why hasn't she gone home yet? You and Claud must know how much I worried about you. But one thing I learned about this weekend is that adults in my family don't trust me as much as I thought they did.''

Me — ''I am going to try hard to be the laid-back kind of person everyone thinks I am. But I guess I need to know that there are some situations that I don't handle as well as others. I have limits like everyone else.''

Mallory — ''I'm glad I was able to help out last weekend. Even though our searching turned up what looked like the worst clue of all, I found that I like to be active. It helps me to feel in control.''

Mary Anne — ''You know I hate tape recorders, Sis. I can't be myself. . . . What? . . .

Dawn

This thing's already *on?* . . . Um, well, here is how I read the situation. . . . Talk *normally?* . . . All right. . . . All right. This weekend was probably the worst of my life. I know that becoming stepsisters wasn't easy, but when I thought I'd lost you, I felt like I'd lost me, too. I love you, Sis.''

Here are a few final bits of information that helped me put the story of the disaster weekend together.

Dear Stacey,
Thank you for your letter. I'm sure it was not easy to write, and I'm happy that you decided to send it anyway. By now, you probably know that your mother and I have spoken. Stacey, we will try our hardest not to put you in the middle anymore. We don't mean to do that. And how about if I also try to

be more flexible
about which weekends
you spend in New York
and which ones you
spend in Stoneybrook?
You're right. Your time
is yours. Also, from
now on, I will keep in
mind what you said
about being a divorced
kid. I hadn't looked
at your situation quite
that way, but it's a good
way to describe it, and
it puts things in
perspective for me.
                    Lots of love,
                              Dad

Dear Mom, Dawn, Richard,
    and Mary Anne,
    I got home fine. The plane ride was
fun. Even though I fell asleep and
missed the food. Now I'm back in school
but hardly anybuddy beleves what
happenned to me. Can you send a copy
of the newspaper artikle out here please.
                    Love,
                        Jeff

Dawn

Dear Rebecca,
I hope you have recovered from your misadventure. I think of you and Jessica and your brother often. Are you sleeping well? Your father tells me you are back in school again, so that is surely a good sign. I am still thinking of returning to Stoneybrook permanently, so perhaps I shall see you soon.
(The letter goes on, but it is really, really boring.)
Best,
Your Aunt Cecelia

Dear Claudia and Dawn,
Thank you for taking care of me on the island.
Love, JAMIE

I guess all I need to add here is a quote from one of my favorite movies: "There's no place like home!"

226

About the Author

ANN M. MARTIN did *a lot* of baby-sitting when she was growing up in Princeton, New Jersey. Now her favorite baby-sitting charge is her cat, Mouse, who lives with her in her Manhattan apartment.

Ann Martin's Apple Paperbacks include *Yours Turly, Shirley*; *Ten Kids, No Pets*; *With You and Without You*; *Bummer Summer*; and all the other books in the Baby-sitters Club series.

She is a former editor of books for children, and was graduated from Smith College. She likes ice cream, the beach, and *I Love Lucy*; and she hates to cook.

THE BABY-SITTERS CLUB®

by Ann M. Martin

More titles... ▶

The Baby-sitters Club titles continued...

Available wherever you buy books...or use this order form.

Scholastic Inc., P.O. Box 7502, 2931 E. McCarty Street, Jefferson City, MO 65102

Please send me the books I have checked above. I am enclosing $ _____
(please add $2.00 to cover shipping and handling). Send check or money order - no
cash or C.O.D.s please.

Name _____

Address _____

City_____ State/Zip _____

Please allow four to six weeks for delivery. Offer good in the U.S. only. Sorry, mail orders are not
available to residents of Canada. Prices subject to change.

BSC1291

Don't miss out!

Join the BABY-SITTERS Fan Club!

Pssst... Know what? You can find out **everything** there is to know about *The Baby-sitters Club*. Join the BABY-SITTERS FAN CLUB! Get the hot news on the series, the inside scoop on all the Baby-sitters, and lots of baby-sitting fun...just for $4.95!

With your **two-year** membership, you get:

- ☆ An official membership card!
- ☆ A colorful banner!
- ☆ The exclusive Baby-sitters Fan Club quarterly newsletter with baby-sitting tips, activities and more!

Just fill in the coupon below and mail with payment to:
THE BABY-SITTERS FAN CLUB,
Scholastic Inc., P.O. Box 7500, 2931 E. McCarty Street, Jefferson City, MO 65012.

- -

The Baby-sitters Fan Club

❏ **YES!** Enroll me in The Baby-sitters Fan Club! I've enclosed my check or money order (no cash please) for $4.95 made payable to Scholastic Inc.

Name _____ Age _____

Street _____

City _____ State/Zip _____

Where did you buy this *Baby-sitters Club* book?

- ❏ Bookstore
- ❏ Drugstore
- ❏ Supermarket
- ❏ Book Club
- ❏ Book Fair
- ❏ Other_____(specify)

Not available outside of U.S. and Canada.

BSC791

LITTLE 🍎 APPLE®

BABY-SITTERS

Little Sister™

by Ann M. Martin, author of *The Baby-sitters Club*®

Available wherever you buy books, or use this order form.

SLEEPOVER FRIENDS™
by Susan Saunders

☐ MF40641-8	#1 Patti's Luck	$2.50	☐ MF43189-7	#29 Kate the Boss	$2.50
☐ MF40642-6	#2 Starring Stephanie!	$2.50	☐ MF43929-4	#30 Big Sister Stephanie	$2.75
☐ MF40643-4	#3 Kate's Surprise	$2.50	☐ MF43928-6	#31 Lauren's AfterSchool Job	$2.75
☐ MF40644-2	#4 Patti's New Look	$2.50	☐ MF43927-8	#32 A Valentine for Patti!	$2.75
☐ MF41336-8	#5 Lauren's Big Mix-Up	$2.50	☐ MF43926-X	#33 Lauren's Double Disaster	$2.75
☐ MF42816-0	#20 Lauren in the Middle	$2.50	☐ MF43925-1	#34 Kate the Winner	$2.75
☐ MF42817-9	#21 Starstruck Stephanie	$2.50	☐ MF43924-3	#35 The New Stephanie	$2.75
☐ MF42818-7	#22 The Trouble with Patti	$2.50	☐ MF44354-2	#36 Presenting Patti!	$2.75
☐ MF42819-5	#23 Kate's Surprise Visitor	$2.50	☐ MF44355-0	#37 Lauren Saves the Day	$2.75
☐ MF43194-3	#24 Lauren's New Friend	$2.50	☐ MF43923-5	Super Beach Mystery Sleepover Friends Super Special #1	$2.75
☐ MF43193-5	#25 Stephanie and the Wedding	$2.50	☐ MF42662-1	Sleepover Friends' Super Sleepover Guide	$2.50
☐ MF43192-7	#26 The New Kate	$2.50			
☐ MF43190-0	#27 Where's Patti?	$2.50			
☐ MF43191-9	#28 Lauren's New Address	$2.50			

Available wherever you buy books...or use this order form.

Scholastic Inc. P.O. Box 7502, 2931 E. McCarty Street, Jefferson City, MO 65102

Please send me the books I have checked above. I am enclosing $_____

(please add $2.00 to cover shipping and handling). Send check or money order—no cash or C.O.D.s please.

Name _____

Address _____

City_____ State/Zip _____

Please allow four to six weeks for delivery. Offer good in U.S.A. only. Sorry, mail orders are not available to residents of Canada. Prices subject to change.

SF1190